The Alpha Rancher

A Protective Alpha Fated Mates Steamy Age Gap Omegaverse Romance

Ash Jade

D ear Reader,

Welcome to Sanctuary, a hidden mountain town whispered about in the wider omegaverse, a place where worn-down omegas come to heal and alphas learn that strength is measured in gentleness, not dominance. If you've made it this far, maybe part of you is curious... or hopeful... or simply ready to step into a world where instinct doesn't have to hurt, and where every story bends toward safety, connection, and a well-earned happily-ever-after.

Here, the omegaverse works a little differently.

Alphas, betas, and omegas still move through life guided by pheromones, instincts, and bonds, but Sanctuary is a refuge, one carved out of grief, rebuilt with stubborn hope, and held together by a pack that refuses to let anyone fall through the cracks. Heats and ruts still come like wild weather, but they're met with care, consent, and hands that steady instead of seize. And sometimes, the mountain air carries something more ancient still: the pull of fated mates, that quiet click inside your chest when you realize home might be a person as much as a place.

Each novella in this series is a fast, high-heat, heart-forward escape. A story about a protective alpha, a brave omega, and the slow re-teaching of trust. You can read them in order or wander in wherever you like. Every couple stands alone, yet each book threads another stitch into the found-family tapestry of Sanctuary.

Before you step inside, a few gentle warnings:

These stories contain explicit sexual content, primal dynamics, instinct-driven tension, and adult themes. They are not dark romance, but they *do* explore trauma recovery, vulnerability, and the process of learning to choose yourself again. Please honor your comfort level and step away if something doesn't sit right with you.

Additional content considerations: violence, injury, death, mentions of sexual violence (not depicted but discussed), and themes of healing from past harm.

If Sanctuary sounds like somewhere you might want to linger—if you're ready for protective alphas, fierce omegas, small-town gossip, soft pack dinners, and bonds that bloom where hurt once lived—then settle in.

The mountains are waiting.
— Ash Jade

Contents

1

The engine dies with a pathetic wheeze, and my heart sinks as our ancient Honda rolls to a stop on this godforsaken mountain road. "No, no, no," I mutter, twisting the key frantically, the dash lights flickering before blinking out entirely. Rain hammers the roof like angry fists, and through the fogged windshield, nothing but pitch black forest stretches in all directions. My hands tighten on the wheel until my knuckles go white. Three days of running, and this is how it ends—stranded in the middle of nowhere with my heat threatening to break through the suppressants and two terrified pups looking to me for salvation.

"Anna?" Mia's voice from the backseat is small, barely audible above the downpour. "What's happening?"

I swallow hard, forcing calm into my scent. Can't let them smell my panic. "Just car trouble. We'll figure it out."

A lie. This rust bucket was on borrowed time the moment we stole it from the pack garage. I slam my palm against the steering wheel, a growl escaping my throat.

"Is he going to find us?" Liam whispers from beside Mia, his eleven-year-old frame curled tight against his sister. Even in the darkness, I can see the shadow of a bruise on his cheek—Daniel's parting gift.

"No," I say with more conviction than I feel. "We're too far now." Another lie. Daniel has resources, connections. A determined alpha can track a wayward omega across state lines if he's motivated enough. And he is. Property doesn't just walk away in his world.

I check my phone. Dead. Of course it's dead.

The rain intensifies, drumming against the metal roof like artillery fire. We can't stay here. The temperature's dropping, and we've got nothing but the clothes on our backs and a half-empty box of granola bars.

"We need to move," I announce, reaching for the backpack stuffed with what little we managed to grab. "I saw lights down in the valley. Could be a town or a farm. Either way, it's shelter."

"But it's pouring," Mia protests, fourteen going on forty. She's been the practical one since Mom died.

"And it'll be freezing by morning if we stay here." I twist to face them, fixing both with the look that means I'm not arguing. "We stick together. We move fast. We find help."

Liam's shivering already. I peel off my jacket—the good leather one I saved three months to buy—and drape it over his shoulders. It swallows him whole.

"Anna, you need—"

"I run hot," I cut Mia off. Another lie. My omega body craves warmth, especially with my cycle approaching. But I've got enough meat on my bones to survive a little rain. "Let's go."

The moment I open the door, the storm hits me with a physical blow. We're higher in elevation than I realized, the air thin and sharp in my lungs. The mountain looms black against the night sky, occasional lightning illuminating jagged pines that claw at the clouds.

Mia clutches her backpack to her chest, eyes wide and frightened. Liam's hand finds mine, small fingers gripping with desperate strength. I breathe in their scents—milk and honey for Mia, pine sap for Liam—and let my protective instincts surge to the surface. Not as strong as an alpha's, but an omega defending pups is no joke either.

"Stay close," I shout over the wind, pointing down the winding road. "Those lights. That's our target."

We stumble forward, the steep descent making each step treacherous on rain-slicked asphalt. My sneakers are soaked through within minutes, jeans plastered to my legs. Mia's teeth are chattering, and Liam's crying silently, tears mixing with raindrops.

"Almost there," I lie again. The lights are deceptively distant, like stars you can never quite reach.

A mile passes, then maybe another. Time stretches like taffy, measured in shivers and soggy footsteps. The road gives way to gravel, then dirt. We're off the main route now, some forest service track that might lead to salvation or deeper into wilderness. My omega instincts scream danger with every step into unknown territory, but turning back isn't an option.

"I'm tired," Liam mumbles, stumbling against my side.

I crouch down. "Climb on, pup."

He doesn't argue, wrapping thin arms around my neck. I hoist him up piggyback style, his weight a comforting anchor as we press on. He smells of fear sweat and childhood, that particular sweetness not yet sharpened by puberty.

Mia walks silently beside me, stubborn independence in the set of her jaw. She's not presenting yet, but I can already sense the alpha brewing beneath her skin. She'll be a fighter, that one. If we survive long enough to see it.

"You think they'll help us?" she finally asks, voice nearly lost in the storm. "Whoever's down there?"

I adjust Liam, who's growing heavier by the minute. "People help stranded travelers. Especially kids."

"But we're..." She doesn't finish. Doesn't need to.

We're pack rejects. Omegas and pre-designation pups fleeing alpha territory. In some places, that makes us fair game, not worthy of protection. I've heard the stories. We all have.

"This is different," I insist, though I have no way of knowing that. The map I stole from Daniel's office had Sanctuary marked on it—supposedly a haven town for our kind. But maps can lie, and hopes can break. "Just let me do the talking."

The track widens, trees thinning out enough to reveal a sprawling property below us. Through sheets of rain, I make out a large house, a barn, and what might be other outbuildings. A ranch, by the look of it, isolated from whatever town might lie beyond.

A prickle runs up my spine—omega intuition firing warning shots. Big, isolated property means an established alpha. Territorial. Probably dangerous.

But Liam's shivering against my back, and Mia's lips have taken on a bluish tinge.

"We'll just ask to use a phone," I say, as much to convince myself as them. "Get someone to look at the car. We won't mention... anything else."

Lightning cracks overhead, illuminating the ranch in stark relief. For just a moment, I catch sight of a figure moving near the barn—tall, broad-shouldered, unmistakably alpha even at this distance. My steps falter.

"Anna?" Mia tugs my sleeve. "What's wrong?"

Everything. Everything's wrong. But we're out of options.

"Nothing," I say, squaring my shoulders and tightening my grip on Liam. "Just stay behind me when we get there."

The scent of alpha territory grows stronger as we descend, mixing with petrichor and pine. My feet move forward on instinct now, carrying precious cargo toward uncertain shelter. The rain lessens to a steady drizzle as we approach the property line, marked by a weathered fence and cattle gate.

A sign swings from the post, words barely visible in the gloom: "Hawthorne Ranch — Private Property."

I hesitate at the boundary, every omega instinct screaming to turn back. Entering alpha territory uninvited is asking for trouble. But the warm glow from the distant windows calls to us like a beacon, promising safety my body desperately craves.

"It'll be okay," I whisper, though I'm not sure who I'm trying to convince anymore.

Taking a deep breath, I push open the gate and step across the threshold, Mia's hand clutched tightly in mine and Liam's heartbeat steady against my back. The heavy scent of alpha washes over me immediately, primitive and powerful.

Whatever happens next, there's no going back.

2

The alpha's scent hits me before we reach the front porch—pine sap, wood smoke, and something dangerously wild, like gunpowder. My steps falter, instinct screaming at me to grab the pups and run. But there's nowhere to go, and Liam's dead weight on my back reminds me we're out of options. The ranch house looms before us, weathered timber and stone, windows glowing amber against the storm-black sky. A fortress. The door swings open before I can knock, and he fills the frame entirely—six-foot-something of coiled muscle and barely contained aggression, eyes cutting through the darkness to assess the bedraggled omegas trespassing on his land.

"You're on private property." His voice is gravel and thunder, deep enough to vibrate in my chest.

I straighten my spine despite the weight of Liam on my back. "I'm sorry to intrude. Our car broke down a few miles up the mountain." Water drips from my hair into my eyes, and I resist the urge to wipe it away. Can't show weakness. "We just need to use a phone."

His gaze rakes over us—me with a child clinging to my back, Mia shivering beside me, all of us soaked to the bone. In the porch light, I can see him clearly now. Older than me, maybe late thirties, with dark hair cropped military-short at the sides, longer on top. A scar bisects his left eyebrow, another traces his jawline. He wears flannel and worn jeans like a second skin, and his forearms, crossed over his chest, are corded with muscle.

"Town's another eight miles." He doesn't move from the doorway. "Sheriff might help you there."

"Please," Mia speaks up, her voice small but determined. "My brother's really cold."

As if on cue, Liam coughs against my shoulder, a pitiful sound that tightens my chest. The alpha's nostrils flare, scenting us. His eyes narrow on Liam, then back to me.

And that's when it happens.

A current snaps between us, electric and undeniable. His pupils dilate, jaw clenching so hard I can almost hear his teeth grind. My own body betrays me, warmth flooding my core, my scent glands tingling at my throat and wrists. Recognition—primal and absolute.

Oh fuck.

Mate.

His scent changes, deepening with notes of cedar and musk that make my knees weak. I watch him battle it, muscles tensed like he's physically fighting the pull. I'm doing the same, forcing my omega instincts down, down, down where they can't compromise the safety I've fought so hard to secure.

"You're running from something." Not a question. His voice has roughened further, like it's being dragged over broken glass.

I lift my chin. "Someone. Yes."

"Another alpha." Again, not a question.

"Not mine," I spit the words like poison. "Never mine."

He studies me, conflict raging in eyes the color of storm clouds. Behind him, the house beckons with warmth and shelter. Behind us, only darkness and rain.

"Please," I say again, hating the desperation in my voice. "Just for tonight. We'll be gone by morning."

Liam whimpers against my neck, his small body trembling. The alpha's gaze shifts to him, something complicated passing over his face.

"You got names?" he finally asks.

"Annabelle." I hesitate, then nod to the children. "This is Mia, and Liam on my back."

He doesn't offer his in return, just steps back from the doorway. Not an invitation, exactly, but not a refusal.

"There's a bunkhouse out back where the seasonal hands stay." He jerks his chin toward a smaller building visible beyond the main house. "Empty this time of year."

Relief floods me, but I don't move yet. "And you are...?"

"Silas Hawthorne." He says it like the name should mean something. Maybe it does, in these parts. "This is my ranch."

I shift Liam higher on my back, wincing as my muscles protest. "Thank you, Mr. Hawthorne."

"Silas." He corrects me sharply, then looks immediately annoyed at himself for doing so. The mate pull working on him too, forcing intimacy neither of us wants.

Mia edges closer to me, her young face suspicious. Smart girl. Alphas don't offer help without wanting something in return—that's the first lesson any omega learns.

Silas seems to read her thoughts. "I'm not in the habit of turning children away in a storm." He steps fully outside, and I flinch backwards instinctively. He notices, jaw tightening. "Follow me. I'll show you where you can dry off."

He moves past us down the porch steps, keeping a deliberate distance. Each step he takes wafts his scent toward me—that dangerous pine-and-gunpowder blend that makes my glands ache. My body knows what my mind refuses to accept: this man is my biological match. The universe's sick joke after I've just escaped one alpha's clutches.

I follow him anyway, Mia clutching my free hand. The rain has slowed to a drizzle, but the night air bites through my wet clothes. Silas leads us around the main house toward a smaller structure, single-story with a covered porch. His movements are precise, efficient. Military, I'm guessing, from the rigid set of his shoulders and the watchful way he scans the perimeter as we walk.

"Ex-army?" I ask, the words slipping out before I can stop them.

He glances back, surprised. "Marines."

I nod. That explains the haircut, the scars, the hyperawareness. Daniel had ex-military in his pack too—the dangerous ones he sent for "collections."

"I'm not him," Silas says suddenly, stopping at the bunkhouse door. "Whoever you're running from."

My spine stiffens. "I didn't say you were."

"Didn't have to." He unlocks the door, pushing it open. "Your scent says plenty."

Inside, the bunkhouse is simple but clean—four sets of bunks along one wall, a small kitchenette, a bathroom door visible in the back. Silas moves to a closet, pulling out towels and blankets.

"Water's hot. Kitchen's stocked with basics." He places everything on the nearest bed, careful not to come too close. "Main house is locked after ten. Don't try to enter."

I ease Liam down onto the bed. He's half-asleep, exhaustion overriding fear. Mia immediately sits beside him, pulling a blanket around both their shoulders.

"Thank you," I say again, meaning it despite my wariness. "We won't be any trouble."

Silas's eyes find mine, holding for a beat too long. The air between us thickens, that damnable pull tugging like invisible strings. He breaks it first, turning toward the door.

"I'll check your car tomorrow," he says gruffly. "First light."

Then he's gone, door closing firmly behind him. Only his scent remains, clinging to the air like a promise or a threat—I'm not sure which.

Mia looks up at me, eyes too knowing for fourteen. "He's an alpha."

"Yes," I answer, moving to lock the door.

"But not like Daniel."

I think of Silas's restraint, the way he kept his distance despite the biological imperative clawing at us both. The way he looked at Liam with something almost like concern.

"No," I admit. "Not like Daniel."

But that doesn't make him safe. Nothing is safe for omegas on the run, especially not the false security of a mate bond we never asked for.

I pull Liam's shoes off, then help Mia with her soaked jacket. My hands are steady, but inside, everything trembles—with cold, with fear, with the unwelcome heat that flooded me when Silas Hawthorne's eyes met mine.

We've found shelter for the night. Whether we've found sanctuary remains to be seen.

3

Morning light streams through uncurtained windows, illuminating dust motes dancing in golden beams. I've been awake for hours, listening to Mia and Liam breathe, mapping escape routes, counting our meager supplies. The bunkhouse is warmer than expected, the beds surprisingly comfortable. Dangerous comfort. The kind that makes you lower your guard. I slide from beneath the blankets, muscles protesting yesterday's trek, and peer out the window at Hawthorne Ranch in daylight. Sprawling pastures roll toward distant mountains, cattle dots on green velvet. A horse paddock sits empty beside the weathered barn. The main house—Silas's domain—stands like a sentinel, smoke curling from the chimney. As if summoned by my thoughts, the door swings open and he emerges, moving with that contained power that screams predator, that makes my traitor body hum with awareness. He pauses, head lifting, and turns directly toward my window. Even at this distance, I feel the weight of his gaze.

I step back, heart hammering.

"Anna?" Liam's sleepy voice calls from his bunk. "Where are we?"

"Safe place," I answer, turning away from the window. "Just for a little while."

"I'm hungry," he mumbles, rubbing his eyes. His dark hair stands in sleep-wild tufts, making him look younger than eleven.

"Me too," Mia chimes in, already sitting up and assessing our surroundings with sharp eyes. "Did that alpha say we could use the kitchen?"

The "that alpha" makes me smile despite everything. Mia's developing the healthy wariness all omegas need to survive. "He said it's stocked with basics. Let's see what that means."

The kitchen yields more than I expected—eggs, bacon, bread, canned goods, even fresh fruit. We make breakfast in companionable silence, a routine we perfected long ago. The familiarity of it—Liam setting mismatched plates on the small table, Mia scrambling eggs, me brewing coffee strong enough to stand a spoon in—creates a bubble of normalcy in this strange situation.

A knock at the door shatters it.

"Stay here," I murmur, wiping my hands on a dish towel. Through the window, I see Silas waiting on the porch, a box in his arms.

When I open the door, his scent rolls over me like a physical force—stronger in the morning light, sharper with what might be rut hormones simmering beneath the surface. My own body responds instantly, glands at my neck and wrists warming, my core clenching with primitive need. Fucking biology.

"Brought supplies," he says, his voice deliberately neutral. "Clothes, toiletries. Stuff the kids might need."

He thrusts the box forward, careful to keep space between us. His eyes never quite meet mine, instead focusing on a point just past my shoulder. Fighting the pull, same as me.

"Thank you." I take the box, our fingers brushing for a millisecond. Electric. "That's... very kind."

"Not kindness. Practicality." His jaw works. "Your car's shot. Transmission's fried, among other things. I called Colt from town to tow it to his garage, but parts could take a week, minimum."

My stomach drops. "A week? We can't—"

"You can stay until it's fixed." He cuts me off, still not meeting my eyes. "Bunkhouse is empty until spring anyway."

"We can't impose—"

"It's not an imposition if I'm offering." Now he does look at me, storm-gray eyes intense. "Unless you've got somewhere else to go?"

I don't answer. We both know I don't.

"That's what I thought." He nods toward the main house. "I work from sunup to sundown. Stay out of my way, keep the kids from causing trouble, we'll get along fine."

Before I can respond, a whoop of delight sounds from inside the bunkhouse, followed by Liam's excited voice: "Look! He brought us clothes!"

Silas's expression doesn't change, but something softens minutely around his eyes. "There's a creek runs through the back property. Good fishing. Kids might like it." He steps back. "Boots in the box should fit the boy. Gets muddy after rain."

With that, he turns and strides away, leaving me clutching the box of unexpected generosity, confusion and gratitude warring in my chest.

Days settle into an uneasy pattern. Silas works his ranch—fixing fences, tending cattle, splitting wood for coming winter. The children and I keep to ourselves, though Mia and Liam grow bolder each day, venturing further from the bunkhouse to explore.

They discover the horses first—three gentle giants in the back paddock that Silas says are retired from working cattle. Liam forms an immediate bond with the oldest, a chestnut mare named Penny who nuzzles his pockets for treats.

"Can I ride her?" he asks Silas on the third day, eyes wide with hope.

I tense, ready to intervene, but Silas surprises me.

"Tomorrow," he says gruffly. "If it doesn't rain. And if your sister says it's okay."

He looks to me for confirmation, a small but significant acknowledgment of my authority over the children. I nod, throat tight with unexpected emotion.

The chickens are Mia's domain. She collects eggs each morning, talks to the hens like old friends, keeps meticulous count of their laying patterns. Silas shows her how to check for predator signs around the coop, then leaves her to it, as if trusting her completely.

I find myself drawn to the garden—rows of late-season vegetables still producing despite the chill. There's comfort in the mindless work of weeding, harvesting, preparing soil for winter. Sometimes I feel Silas watching from a distance, his gaze a physical touch on my skin.

On the fifth day, I corner him by the woodpile. "We can't keep taking without giving back," I say, forcing myself to meet those storm-cloud eyes. "Let me help around the ranch. I'm stronger than I look."

His gaze flicks over me—assessing, not leering. "The garden," he finally says. "Winter prep needs doing. And the preserving."

"I can handle that." I hesitate. "And I want to pay you. When the car's fixed—"

"No." The word is sharp, final. "Money's not the issue here."

"Then what is?"

He splits a log with one powerful swing, muscles bunching beneath his flannel shirt. "You being here at all."

The words sting, though I have no right to feel hurt. We're strangers, unwanted guests at best. "We'll be gone as soon as possible."

"That's not—" He drives the axe into the chopping block with unnecessary force. "That's not what I meant."

"Then what did you mean?"

He doesn't answer, just wipes sweat from his brow with a forearm. Up close, I can see more scars than I initially noticed—thin white lines on his knuckles, a jagged one disappearing beneath his collar. Warrior marks.

"Dinner," he says abruptly. "At the house tonight. Seven o'clock."

I blink. "What?"

"Dinner," he repeats, not looking at me. "You. The kids. Proper meal at a proper table."

"Why?"

Now he does look at me, something complicated and fierce in his expression. "Because they're children who've been running scared, and they deserve one damn night of normal."

The invitation hangs between us, weighted with implications neither of us is ready to acknowledge.

"Okay," I say finally. "Seven o'clock."

That evening, we sit at Silas's dining table—heavy oak worn smooth by generations of use. The meal is simple but plentiful: roast chicken, potatoes, vegetables from the garden I've been tending. Liam chatters about the horses, Mia describes her chicken-monitoring system. Silas listens more than he speaks, but his attention never wavers.

I watch him across the table, this contradiction of a man—gruff yet gentle, distant yet attentive. The more I learn, the more dangerous he becomes to my resolve. Because kindness from an alpha is far more seductive than force could ever be.

After the children are tucked into their bunks, I stand on the porch, staring at the stars scattered like salt across the black velvet sky. The night air carries Silas's scent from the main house—that pine-and-gunpowder blend that makes my body ache with recognition.

A week has stretched to nearly two. The car sits in town, waiting on parts that seem perpetually delayed. Each day the children sink deeper roots into this temporary soil. Each day the tension between Silas and me grows thicker, harder to ignore.

And each day, I feel my carefully constructed walls developing hairline cracks, threatening to crumble entirely.

4

October bleeds into November. The car sits forgotten in town, mentioned less frequently in our daily conversations. I tell myself we're just waiting for parts, but the truth hangs in the cooling air—we're stalling. Each morning I wake with the intention of making plans to leave, and each evening I crawl into bed having failed. The bunkhouse no longer feels temporary. Mia's books line the windowsill; Liam's drawings plaster the refrigerator door. My own scent has worked itself into the sheets, the couch, the worn armchair by the fireplace. Worse, it's mingling with traces of Silas that drift in whenever he visits—which is increasingly often, always with some practical excuse that fools neither of us. The children orbit him like planets caught in a gravitational pull, and I watch it happen, torn between terror and a longing so deep it scrapes my bones hollow.

"Anna, look what Silas taught me!" Liam bursts through the door, cheeks flushed with cold and excitement. He's carrying a roughly carved wooden horse, pride radiating from every pore. "He says I'm a natural with the whittling knife."

I examine the figure, genuinely impressed by the recognizable shape. "It's amazing, pup. But a knife? You're only eleven."

"Silas says that's plenty old enough if you're careful. He watched me the whole time." His eyes shine with something I haven't seen in years—pure, uncomplicated happiness. "He says tomorrow we can start on a whole herd."

Behind him, Silas leans against the doorframe, arms crossed over his chest. He's been doing that more lately—lingering, finding reasons to stay close. His eyes meet mine over Liam's head, a silent question there. Seeking approval, maybe. Or permission.

I nod slightly, and something eases in his expression.

"Wash up for dinner," I tell Liam, ruffling his hair. "You smell like sawdust."

When he's gone, Silas steps inside, closing the door against the evening chill. The bunkhouse shrinks immediately, his presence filling every corner. He smells different today—his usual pine-and-gunpowder scent intensified, undercut with musk that makes my inner omega whine with recognition.

Rut hormones. Early stages.

"You didn't have to do that," I say, busying myself with dinner preparations to hide my body's reaction. "Teach him whittling."

"Kid's got talent." Silas moves to the sink, washing his hands with the efficiency of someone used to manual labor. Water darkens the rolled cuffs of his flannel shirt. "And he needed something that was just his. Mia has her chickens. He needed his thing."

The casual insight into my brother's needs catches me off guard. "You notice a lot."

"Hard not to." He dries his hands on a dish towel, careful to maintain distance between us despite the small space. "They're good kids. Smart. Resilient."

"They've had to be." I don't elaborate. He's never pushed for details about our past, and I've never offered them.

"Anna?" Mia calls from outside. "Can you come see? The coop expansion is done!"

I glance at Silas. "Coop expansion?"

He shrugs, almost sheepish. "She wanted more chickens. Made a whole presentation about egg production and sustainability."

"And you just... built it for her?"

"She helped design it. Did most of the hammering herself." Pride colors his voice. "Girl's got a future in engineering if she wants it."

Something warm and dangerous unfurls in my chest. I push past him, needing fresh air, needing distance from the domesticity that threatens to ensnare me.

Outside, Mia stands beside a newly expanded chicken coop, beaming with accomplishment. It's well-built, practical but pretty with a sloped roof and fresh white paint.

"Silas says we can get three more hens at the feed store next week," she announces. "Rhode Island Reds. They're the best winter layers."

"Next week," I echo, the words sticking in my throat. "Mia, we might not be here next week."

Her face falls. Behind me, I sense rather than see Silas tense.

"But why would we leave?" Mia asks, genuine confusion in her voice. "The car isn't fixed yet."

"It will be eventually."

"So?" She gestures around the ranch. "We're safe here. Liam's happy. I'm happy." Her young face grows serious. "You're happy too. I can smell it."

Heat crawls up my neck. Damn secondary gender biology—can't hide anything from another with heightened senses, even a pre-designation pup.

"That's not the point," I say, voice low. "We can't stay forever. This isn't our home."

"It could be," Liam pipes up, appearing from the bunkhouse. "Silas said so."

My head whips around to stare at Silas, who has the grace to look uncomfortable. "Did he now?"

"Not in so many words," Silas says carefully. "We were talking about winter preparations. The boy asked if they'd be here to see the snow."

"And you said?"

His eyes hold mine. "I said that was up to their sister."

The children look at me with such naked hope it physically hurts. I've spent years trying to give them stability, safety, something approaching normal. Here it is on a silver platter, and I'm the one hesitating.

"We'll talk about it later," I deflect, turning toward the bunkhouse. "Dinner's almost ready."

That night, after the children are asleep, I sit on the porch steps, watching clouds slide across the moon. The temperature has dropped sharply, promising frost by morning. I pull my borrowed jacket—Silas's, from his early ranching days, he'd said gruffly—tighter around my shoulders.

His scent wraps around me, a phantom embrace that makes my body hum with awareness. It's stronger than before, edged with the unmistakable notes of pre-rut. My own cycle will follow soon—omega biology syncing to a compatible alpha's rhythm. A dangerous dance we've been avoiding since that first night.

Footsteps crunch on gravel, and Silas appears out of the darkness. He keeps a respectful distance, sitting on the opposite end of the steps. Even in the dim light, I can see the heightened color in his face, the slight sheen of sweat at his temples despite the cold.

"You're going into rut," I say quietly.

He doesn't deny it. "Few days still. I'll stay clear until it passes."

"Do you want us gone? Before you lose control?"

His laugh is harsh, humorless. "If that was what I wanted, you'd be gone already."

"Then what do you want, Silas?"

The question hangs between us, heavy with possibility. He stares out at his land, jaw working.

"Been alone a long time," he finally says. "By choice. After what I saw, what I did overseas..." He shakes his head. "Figured it was better that way."

I wait, sensing he needs to get this out.

"Then you three show up on my doorstep." His voice drops lower. "And suddenly my house is too damn quiet. My table's too empty. My purpose isn't enough anymore."

My heart thunders in my chest. "The children love it here."

"And you?" His eyes find mine in the darkness. "What do you want, Annabelle?"

Safety. Security. A place where Mia can raise chickens and Liam can whittle horses and neither of them flinches when an alpha raises his voice.

"I want what's best for them," I answer honestly.

"That's not what I asked."

No, it isn't. And maybe that's the problem. I've spent so long being what the children need that I've forgotten how to want things for myself.

"I'm scared," I admit, the words barely audible. "Not of you. Of this." I gesture vaguely between us. "Of wanting to stay. Of what happens if we do. Of what happens if we don't."

He nods slowly, understanding in his eyes. "Nothing has to happen that you don't choose, Annabelle. Mate pull or not."

The acknowledgment of what we've both been feeling sends a shiver through me that has nothing to do with the cold.

"And if I choose to leave?" I challenge.

Pain flashes across his face, quickly masked. "Then I help you get where you need to go. Safely."

"And if I choose to stay?"

His scent spikes, filling the space between us with want so thick I could drown in it. "Then you stay on your terms. Not mine. Not biology's."

I look toward the bunkhouse where my siblings sleep, then back to the man whose quiet strength has become our unexpected sanctuary.

"Let me think about it," I say finally.

He rises, and I catch the slight tremor in his hands—rut symptoms advancing faster than he'd admitted. "Take all the time you need. I'm not going anywhere."

As he walks away, his scent lingers, calling to something primal in me. My body knows what it wants, has from the first moment. My mind is slower to trust, to believe that safety and desire could exist in the same space.

Behind me, the bunkhouse sits warm and welcoming. Ahead, Silas disappears into his home alone. Between us stretches possibility, terrifying and beautiful in equal measure.

5

—·—

Silas returns from the north pasture with a face like thunder. I spot him from the garden where I'm pulling the last of the root vegetables before frost can claim them. Something in his posture—shoulders rigid, movements clipped—sends alarm bells ringing through my system. He scans the property in deliberate sweeps, eyes lingering on the tree line, the road, the spaces between outbuildings. A predator sensing intrusion. I drop the half-filled basket, wiping dirt on my jeans as I intercept his path to the house.

"What is it?" I ask, voice low so the children, collecting eggs by the coop, can't hear.

He meets my eyes, and the cold fury there makes my blood freeze.

"Someone's been watching the property," he says. "And they smell like you—like family."

My heart stutters. "How long?"

"Scent's fresh. Last night, maybe early morning." His nostrils flare, rut-heightened senses picking up my fear. "Who is it, Annabelle?"

I glance toward Mia and Liam, blissfully unaware as they feed chickens, their laughter carrying on the crisp air.

"Not here," I murmur. "Please."

He nods once, sharply, and leads me to the barn. Inside, the space feels too small, his agitated scent filling every corner. Pre-rut pheromones mingle with protective rage—a dangerous combination that makes my knees weak for entirely different reasons.

"Talk," he demands, voice rough with strain.

"They're from my old pack," I admit, arms wrapping around myself. "Daniel's enforcers. He doesn't let anyone leave, especially not omegas."

"Daniel." Silas tests the name, disgust evident. "The alpha you said was never yours."

"He tried to make me his." The words taste like ash. "After our parents died, he took us in—me, Mia, Liam. Said he was honoring pack bonds. But once I turned twenty-one, presented fully as omega…" I swallow hard. "He decided I'd be his next mate."

Silas's hands clench into fists. "Did he—"

"No," I cut him off. "Not for lack of trying. I was… careful. Made sure we were never alone. Then he started looking at Mia—she hasn't presented yet, but he said he could smell the alpha in her. Said she'd need 'special training' to learn her place."

A growl builds in Silas's chest, so deep I feel it vibrate in my own ribcage.

"We left that night," I finish. "Stole a pack car, grabbed what we could carry. Been running ever since."

"How many would he send?"

"Two, maybe three. The Twins—Brian and Brady—they're his trackers. Ex-military like you, but dishonorable discharges. They enjoy the hunt." My voice cracks. "If they found us..."

Silas moves suddenly, crossing to a large metal cabinet in the corner. He unlocks it, revealing an arsenal that would make most preppers jealous—shotguns, rifles, handguns, even what looks like military-grade combat gear.

"You've been to war before," he says, not a question.

"Not like you have."

He checks a shotgun with practiced ease, then a handgun. "Different battlefields, same stakes." He hands me the pistol, grip first. "You know how to use this?"

I take it, the weight familiar. "Daniel insisted all pack members learn. Said it was for protection."

"Control," Silas corrects. "But useful now."

He moves with frightening efficiency, grabbing ammunition, extra weapons, what might be motion sensors. His military training surfaces in his methodical preparations, the way he prioritizes defensive positions.

"The children stay close to the house," he orders. "No more wandering. No more chicken coop unless one of us is with them. Windows locked, doors secured."

"They'll ask questions."

"Then answer them." His eyes meet mine, hard but not unkind. "They're old enough to know when they're in danger."

He's right, of course. I've been protecting them from the truth as much as from Daniel. Maybe too much.

Within hours, Silas has transformed the property. Motion sensors at strategic points, extra locks on doors and windows. He moves the horses from the far pasture to the paddock near the house, explaining that animals make excellent early warning systems.

I watch him secure our perimeter with the calm precision of someone who's done this before. Protected others before. Fought before.

"You were what—Force Recon?" I ask as he adjusts a sensor.

He glances up, surprised. "How'd you know?"

"The way you move. The preparedness. The thousand-yard stare sometimes." I shrug. "My father served. Not special forces, but he told me how to recognize the type."

Something shifts in Silas's expression—respect, maybe. "Three tours. Didn't talk about it much when I got back."

"You don't have to now."

His hands still on the sensor. "This isn't my first time protecting people, Annabelle. It won't be my last." The unspoken message hangs between us: I won't let them take you.

By evening, the property is as secure as Silas can make it. I gather the children in the bunkhouse, Silas standing silent sentry by the door as I explain the situation in simplified terms.

"Bad people from our old pack might be looking for us," I tell them. "We need to be extra careful for a while."

Liam's eyes widen, but there's no real fear there—just the excitement of a child playing a new game. "Like spies?" he asks.

"Not spies, pup. These people want to hurt us."

Mia, sharper and more aware, connects the dots immediately. "It's Daniel, isn't it? He's found us."

The name drops like a stone in still water. Liam's excitement vanishes, replaced by the haunted look I've tried so hard to erase.

"We don't know for sure," I hedge. "But Silas found signs someone's been watching the ranch."

"He'll kill them if they try to take us, right?" Liam looks to Silas with complete trust, and something in my chest cracks at the sight.

Silas meets the boy's gaze steadily.

"Nobody's taking you anywhere you don't want to go," he promises, voice low and certain. "This is my land. My rules."

The fierceness in his tone should frighten me—this lethal capability lurking beneath his controlled exterior. Instead, it soothes something primal in my omega brain that craves protection, security, strength.

And that terrifies me more than Daniel's enforcers.

Later, after the children are asleep, I stand under the shower's hot spray, trying to wash away the day's tension. My skin feels too tight, hypersensitive to the water's caress. The base of my spine aches with a familiar pressure, and slick dampens my thighs despite my fear.

My heat, approaching faster than expected. Stress and proximity to a compatible alpha accelerating my cycle.

The worst possible timing.

I press my forehead against the cool tile, fighting the fever I feel building in my blood. The suppressants I've been taking since we fled are wearing off—I have only two pills left, saved for emergency use. Is this emergency enough? Or should I wait until we see actual proof of Daniel's men?

A soft knock at the bathroom door startles me.

"Anna?" Silas calls, voice muffled. "Need to check the perimeter one more time. Stay inside, keep the door locked."

"I will," I call back, wincing at the husky quality of my voice.

A pause. "You okay in there?"

No. I'm terrified. I'm exhausted. I'm fighting my own body's demands. And underneath it all, I want nothing more than to let you claim me, protect me, take this burden from my shoulders just for a little while.

"Fine," I lie. "Just tired."

Another pause, longer this time. I can almost feel him scenting the air, catching hints of my changing chemistry even through the door.

"Get some rest," he finally says. "I'll be close by all night."

His footsteps retreat, and I sink to the shower floor, water pounding on my shoulders. Outside, danger stalks the boundaries of our temporary haven. Inside, my own biology betrays me with every passing hour.

I'm caught between twin threats—Daniel's enforcers hunting us from without, my omega nature ambushing me from within. And in the middle stands Silas, my unlikely protector, fighting his own battle against rut-driven instincts that call him to claim what his alpha senses insist is already his.

6

M orning arrives with fire in my veins. I wake drenched in sweat, sheets twisted around my legs, the cotton abrasive against hypersensitive skin. Slick pools between my thighs, and every breath draws Silas's lingering scent deeper into my lungs, making me whimper with need. Full-blown heat, impossible to ignore or suppress. I drag myself from bed before the children wake, locking myself in the bathroom to assess the damage. My reflection tells the story—pupils blown wide, cheeks flushed, lips swollen. Glands at my neck and wrists angry-red and throbbing.

I press my forehead against the mirror's cool surface and count the options I don't have. Can't leave the property with Daniel's men lurking. Can't risk exposing the children to an omega in heat. Can't trust any alpha except... him. The thought of Silas sends another wave of slick gushing down my thighs, my body making its preference abundantly clear.

"Fuck," I whisper, voice already wrecked. I fumble through my toiletry bag for the emergency suppressants—two pills that might buy me a few hours at best. Enough time to figure something out. I swallow them dry, gagging slightly as they scrape down my throat.

A knock at the bathroom door nearly makes me jump out of my skin.

"Anna?" Mia calls. "You okay? You're taking forever."

I turn the shower on cold, stepping under the spray fully clothed.

"Fine," I call back, teeth chattering. "Just…not feeling great. Might be coming down with something."

"Want me to get Silas?" Her voice is already laced with concern. "He has medicine in the main house."

"No!" The word comes out too sharp. I soften my tone. "No, sweetie. It's just a—a stomach thing. I'll be fine. Can you and Liam get breakfast started? And maybe stay in the bunkhouse today, okay? Because of the…security concerns."

A pause. "Sure, Anna. Feel better."

I hear her footsteps retreat and slide down the shower wall, letting the cold water numb my overheated skin. It's a temporary fix. I've been through heats before—solo, locked in my room at Daniel's compound, fighting through the agony rather than accepting "help" from alphas I couldn't trust. But this is different. This heat feels nuclear, my body recognizing its genetic match and demanding consummation.

The suppressants might as well be sugar pills.

By mid-morning, I'm delirious with need. Locked in my room, a towel stuffed under the door to contain my scent, I writhe on the bed as cramps tear through my abdomen. Sweat soaks through fresh sheets, and I've resorted to stuffing a washcloth between my legs to contain the endless slick. Every movement of air feels like torture against my skin. Every distant sound like a promise of relief or threat of discovery.

The children knock periodically. I send them away with reassurances that grow weaker by the hour.

"Maybe we should get Silas," I hear Liam suggest outside my door.

"She said not to," Mia responds, but uncertainty colors her voice.

"But she sounds really sick."

I drag a pillow over my face, muffling the whimpers I can no longer control. My hindbrain chants a primal litany: alpha, knot, breed, mate. Biological imperatives I've always prided myself on resisting now consume my every thought.

I need Silas. I need him so badly I could weep.

As if summoned by my desperate thoughts, a new scent cuts through my heat-fog—pine, gunpowder, and raw alpha musk, thick with rut. My body responds instantly, another gush of slick soaking the mattress beneath me.

Heavy footsteps on the porch. A low, rumbling growl that vibrates through the walls.

"Mia," Silas's voice, strained almost beyond recognition. "Take your brother to the main house. Now."

"But Anna's sick—"

"She's not sick." His voice drops even lower. "She's in heat. Go to the house. Food in the fridge. TV in the den. Don't come back to the bunkhouse until I come get you."

A shuffle of movement, murmured questions, the door closing. Then silence, heavy with anticipation.

Three sharp knocks on my bedroom door.

"Annabelle." My name in his mouth sounds like a prayer and a curse combined. "I can smell you through the walls."

I whimper, beyond words.

"Let me in, or tell me to go." His voice is controlled, but just barely. "Your choice. Always your choice."

I drag myself from the bed on trembling limbs, slick running down my thighs, and fumble with the lock. The door swings open.

Silas fills the frame, eyes gone alpha-red, veins standing out on his neck and forearms as he grips the doorframe to keep from reaching for me. His scent hits me like a physical blow—full rut, triggered by my heat. He's fighting it, muscles rigid with the effort of maintaining control.

"Tell me what you want," he grates out.

What I want. No one's asked me that in so long.

"You," I whisper, the admission breaking something loose inside me. "I want you, Silas." Something savage and beautiful crosses his face. "The children are safe in the house. If you're sure—"

"I'm sure." I step toward him on unsteady legs. "Please."

The last thread of his control snaps. He crosses the threshold in one stride, gathering me against him, one hand tangling in my hair as he buries his face in my neck, inhaling deeply at my scent gland.

"Wanted you since that first night," he growls against my skin. "Dreamed of you like this, wet and ready for me."

I moan as his teeth graze my neck, not breaking skin but promising. My hands clutch at his shoulders, his back, anywhere I can reach. Every point of contact burns in the best way, soothing the heat-ache momentarily before stoking it higher.

"Not here," he says suddenly, lifting his head. "Not with their scents all around. Come to my bed."

Before I can respond, he lifts me effortlessly, cradling me against his chest. I should protest—I'm not small, and the main house is a fair distance—but the feeling of being carried by my alpha short-circuits my brain.

My alpha. When did that happen?

The cool November air hits my heated skin as he strides across the yard, but I barely notice, too consumed by the strength of his arms around me, the steady thud of his heart against my ear. He kicks open his front door, not bothering with lights as he carries me through the house to a large bedroom at the back.

His scent is strongest here, concentrated in the sheets he lays me upon. I roll instinctively, pressing my face into his pillow and breathing him in. Behind me, I hear the harsh rasp of his breathing, the rustle of clothing being shed.

"Look at me," he commands softly.

I turn, eyes drinking in the sight of him—all corded muscle and battle scars, cock standing rigid against his abdomen. He's magnificent, this warrior who's become our protector.

"Still your choice," he says, voice rough with need. "Even now."

I reach for him in answer, and he comes to me like a storm breaking, covering my body with his larger frame. His mouth claims mine in a kiss that's all teeth and tongue and desperation, swallowing my moans as his hands explore every inch of me. He strips away my sweat–soaked clothes with efficient movements, growling approval at each new expanse of skin revealed.

When he spreads my thighs and sees the evidence of my need glistening there, his control fractures further.

"So wet," he groans, sliding thick fingers through my folds. "So ready for me."

"Please," I gasp as he works two fingers inside me, my inner walls clenching greedily. "Silas, please, I need—"

He leans over me, caging me in with the solid weight of his body and the heat of his stare, and for a split second I'm sure neither of us is breathing. His cock is already leaking precome, the broad head glossy and flushed, and my hips cant upward—offering, needy, desperate for what my body recognizes as its fate. The blunt nudge at my entrance sends a shudder through me, all the way to my curled toes. He strokes up the length of my thigh, thumbing the slick pooled there, spreading it over my clit in slow, possessive circles that have me gasping and sobbing into the sheets.

"Anna, look at me," he commands, voice gritted and trembling with the effort to hold himself back.

I force my eyes open, lashes sticky with fever-sweat, and meet his gaze. It's not red anymore—not entirely. There's a flicker of blue ringed with that telltale primal glow, a war playing out in real time behind his pupils. For a moment, I wonder if he'll stop, if the part of him that's a good man, a caretaker, will override the wolf. But then he lines himself up, fingers digging into my hips, and sinks in with one slow, inexorable slide.

The invasion is seismic.

He's massive, thicker than any alpha I've ever taken, and the stretch is a sharp burn at first, then a volcanic flood of relief as he pushes past the initial resistance. Every nerve ending in my cunt sparks, the walls spasming around him, drawing him deeper, like my body's trying to drag him straight into my core and fuse us together. I cry out—not in pain, but in something so much more complicated, a sound that's half agony, half gratitude, all animal.

Silas shudders, forehead dropping to the crook of my neck as he holds himself still, letting me adjust. His breaths are harsh and ragged, every exhale ghosting over the bite-scarred skin at my scent gland. He doesn't move, not until I buck against him, greedy for more, greedy for everything.

"You're perfect," he groans, voice hoarse with restraint. "So fucking perfect, Anna. You were made for me."

He starts to move, slow and careful, dragging out until I can feel the ridge of his head catch at my entrance, then pushing back in with a little more force each time. The friction is devastating, my body so wet that every thrust is accompanied by a lewd, slick sound, a chorus to my whimpers and moans. I clutch at his back, nails raking down his spine, and feel the ripple of muscle under my hands as he battles for control.

"Silas, please," I beg, my voice raw, "don't hold back, I need it—I need you to—"

He snarls, a genuine wolf sound that vibrates in his chest and mine, and slams in to the hilt. The bed frame groans under the impact. The force knocks the air out of me, but it's good, it's so fucking good, the fullness and the stretch and the way his knot is already swelling at the base, promising more to come. He fucks me in earnest now, rutting deep and hard, hips snapping against my ass with a violence that should scare me but only makes me wetter, makes me want to open wider for him, let him take everything.

I tilt my head, baring my neck even as I bare myself everywhere else. He gets the message and latches on, teeth scraping my gland in a way that's almost a claim, almost a bite, and I lose the last of my composure. I sob into the pillow, spasming around his cock, desperate to milk him, to be filled, to be knotted and marked as his forever.

"Say it," he growls into my hair, voice breaking. "Say you're mine, Anna."

"I'm yours," I choke out, and it's a plea and a promise and a prayer.

His knot catches on the next thrust, the stretch almost unbearable but I take it, I take all of him, locking us together as he pistons through the last barrier. My orgasm rips through me with the force of a thunderclap, my vision going white at the edges as I clench down on him, milking his knot for every drop. He follows, hips jerking in a staccato rhythm, my name torn from his throat as he empties himself inside me.

We collapse into a tangled, shaking heap, still joined, still caught in the aftershocks. He cradles me to his chest, stroking my hair as if he can soothe the fire he's just stoked to a roaring blaze. I can still feel the pulse of him inside me, the slow, steady throbbing of his cock as it continues to spurt and swell, binding us together more completely than any words could.

The ache doesn't subside; if anything, it intensifies, heightened by the aftershocks of my orgasm and his steady, possessive hold on my body. Even tangled together, still joined, it's not enough. I clutch at him greedily, needing more—the pressure of his weight, the heat of his skin, the pulse of his cock throbbing inside me. My hands roam over the expanse of his shoulders, nails raking down his back, desperate to leave a trace.

I'm still riding the edge, want layered over want until it's almost unbearable. I lock my ankles behind him, drawing him even deeper, grinding against the base of his knot as if I can coax another high from the bare friction alone. Silas groans, shifting to lie beside me, but I whimper at the loss and twist on his cock, refusing to let him go. The fullness keeps me pinned to the present, body lit up with afterglow and anticipation all at once.

He cards his fingers through my hair, gentling me, but I snap at his jaw with my teeth, hungry and wild, barely in control of my own heat-scrambled instincts. I want to consume him—every sound, every scent, every inch of skin. My entire world narrows to the taste of sweat and want on his throat, to the rough scrape of stubble above the bite mark he left.

When his knot finally softens and slips from me, I feel hollowed out, frantic, relentless. I roll him onto his back, straddling his hips before he can even catch his breath. "More," I demand, nails digging crescent moons into his chest. "Harder. I need—" The rest of the words dissolve into a gasp as I guide him back inside, still slick and aching, already fluttering around the thickness of him.

He looks at me as if I'm the only thing he's ever wanted. "Fuck, Anna," he mutters, voice hoarse and reverent, "you're insatiable."

He sits up, one arm banded around my waist, the other hand fisting in my hair as he buries his face in the crook of my neck. "You want it rough?" he growls, barely more than a rumble in my ear. "I'll give you rough." The challenge is magnetic, and I bare my throat, goading him on.

He thrusts up hard, the angle punishing in the best way, cock stretching me open to the brink of pain and then flooding it with pleasure. I ride him, hips snapping, using his body like it's mine by right, and it is, it is, because he gave it to me. Our rhythm is feral, urgent, all instinct and slick and sound. The headboard slams in time with my pulse, the mattress shudders beneath us, but nothing could ever be enough.

He flips us, pinning me beneath him with a growl, and pounds into me with a violence that cracks me open, layer by layer, until I am nothing but nerve endings and need. My cries bounce off the walls, raw and uninhibited, but he's beyond words now, rutting into me like he can't bear to be separate even for a second. His hand presses between my legs, circling my clit with ruthless precision, sending sparks through my bloodstream.

I am a live wire, overloaded, greedy for every scrap of sensation. "Please, Silas," I sob, "don't stop—don't ever—"

He clamps a hand over my mouth and slams into me until I see white, his knot swelling again, battering at my entrance until my body yields, stretching to accommodate the impossible width. The pain is exquisite, the pleasure savage. I claw at his shoulders, desperate for a claim, a mark, anything to make this moment permanent.

Something primal flashes in his eyes.

"Gonna take such good care of you," he promises, then drives home with a thrust that rocks the bed against the wall.

He pounds into me relentlessly, each thrust sparking fireworks behind my eyes. I match his rhythm, hips rising to meet his, taking him deeper with every movement. Our scents mingle and intensify, omega heat and alpha rut creating a feedback loop of escalating pleasure.

"Mine," he growls against my throat, teeth scraping the sensitive gland there. "Say it."

"Yours," I gasp as he hits a spot inside me that makes my vision blur. "I'm yours, Silas."

I can tell he's on the brink of giving in, the urge to bite—to claim—so close to consuming him I taste it as a tang in my own mouth. His teeth graze the soft curve of my neck, lips parted, breath searing hot and uneven, and for a suspended instant I brace for the puncture, the irrevocable. My skin prickles, anticipation racing through my veins as his alpha's heat pulses against my own, every instinct in my body desperate to be marked and made his. His cock throbs, locked tight by the knot swelling inside me, every twitch a reminder that the only thing separating us from forever is the thin membrane of his restraint.

He growls, low and guttural, vibrating straight through my bones, but even as his jaw tenses, he doesn't break the surface. Instead, he sucks hard at my scent gland, drawing blood just beneath the skin, leaving a bruise that aches with promise rather than finality. I shudder and clench around him, greedy for everything he's holding back, but at the last possible edge of self-control, he lets out a strangled sound and mouths a wordless apology into my hair.

We're still fused, bodies shaking, slicked with sweat and release, the room echoing with our ragged gasps and the thrum of desire threatening to reignite at the smallest provocation. His hands convulse on my hips, pinning me so tight I know I'll wear his fingerprints for days. But the pressure is careful, measured, as if even now he's terrified of breaking me, of giving in to the animal that wants to ruin and rebuild me in his image.

The aftershocks are brutal—my body seizes around his knot, milking every drop, every pulse, every ounce of him until I'm dizzy with satisfaction and something rawer, something vulnerable and almost holy. He buries his face in the crook of my neck, holding me through the cresting waves, and I can feel the rapid stutter of his heartbeat against my spine, his chest heaving with the magnitude of what we almost did.

When the shudders finally ebb, he relaxes a fraction, arms circling me in a crushing embrace. I tense for a moment, mind caught up in the old panic of being restrained, but this isn't violence or possession—this is safety, sanctuary, the world narrowing to the circle of his body around mine. I let myself breathe, let myself be held, and the vulnerability is almost more overwhelming than the sex itself.

He whispers my name, a benediction, and I turn to meet his eyes. They're wrecked and red, but there's that ring of blue again, the man fighting the wolf, and for the first time I realize how close I came to being claimed in every sense of the word. I should be afraid, but all I feel is relief, gratitude that he didn't cross that line—not yet, not without my say-so.

We lie tangled and panting, locked together in the most intimate way possible. His weight should feel crushing, but instead feels like an anchor grounding me as heat-tremors continue to ripple through my body. His scent has changed subtly, intertwining with mine to create something new and uniquely ours.

"You okay?" he murmurs against my temple, lips brushing the sweat-damp skin there.

I nod, words beyond me for the moment. My heat hasn't broken—one coupling rarely does the trick—but the desperate edge has dulled to

something more manageable. For now.
His hand strokes down my side, gentling me as his knot slowly begins to recede. Neither of us speaks for a long while, content to breathe each other in, to exist in this moment of perfect biological harmony.

"I should have warned you," he finally says, voice rough with spent passion. "Been edging into rut for days. Tried to fight it."

"Why?" I turn my head to see his face.

"Didn't want you to feel…" He searches for the right word. "Pressured. Or trapped."

The consideration in that statement washes over me like warm water. Most alphas would see an omega's heat as an opportunity, a guaranteed consent. Silas saw it as a complication for me.

"I'm not trapped," I tell him, surprising myself with the certainty in my voice. "This is a choice I'm making. You're a choice I'm making."

His eyes, still tinged with alpha-red, search mine. Whatever he finds there seems to satisfy him, because he nuzzles against my neck again, scenting me thoroughly.

"Rest while you can," he murmurs. "This isn't over yet."

He's right. Already I can feel the heat rising again, slower this time but no less inevitable. My body wants more—more of his touch, his scent, his seed.

For the first time since my designation presented, I surrender willingly to my omega nature, trusting this alpha to guide me through the fire.

7

The sun hangs low on the horizon when I wake, gold light slanting through unfamiliar curtains. Silas's bed, Silas's room. Silas's scent surrounding me like a physical embrace. My heat has ebbed temporarily—the brief respite that comes between waves, allowing omegas to hydrate, eat, regain strength before the next onslaught. My body feels used in the best possible way, pleasantly sore in places that remind me of his possession. He's not beside me, though the sheets still hold his warmth. I stretch languidly, listening for sounds of his movement in the house. Nothing. Then, cutting through the comfortable silence—a low, warning growl from outside, followed by the unmistakable sound of Silas chambering a round.

I bolt upright, instinct overriding discomfort. Something's wrong.

The bedroom door flies open, and Silas stands there, shotgun in hand, expression murderous. He's dressed hastily—jeans, no shirt, bare feet.

His eyes still hold the red tinge of rut, but there's nothing lustful in his gaze now. Pure predator.

"Stay here," he commands, voice pitched low. "Lock the door behind me."

"What's happening?" I'm already moving, pulling on the closest garment—his discarded flannel shirt from earlier.

"Two vehicles just pulled up at the gate." His nostrils flare. "Three men. Unfamiliar, but their scent has your pack markers all over it."

My blood runs cold. "Daniel's men. The Twins—"

"And one more." He crosses to a chest of drawers, pulls out a handgun, checks the clip with practiced ease. "The children are safe. I locked them in the panic room when I heard the first vehicle."

"Panic room?" I blink.

"Reinforced cellar under the kitchen. Military-grade door. They can't get to them." He holds my gaze. "But I need you safe too. Stay here. Lock the door. If anyone but me tries to enter—" He extends the gun.

I take it without hesitation. "I know how to use it."

Something fierce and approving flashes across his face. He pulls me in for a bruising kiss that tastes of possession and promise, then pushes me gently back toward the bed.

"Mine to protect," he growls, and then he's gone, door closing behind him.

I move immediately to lock it, then to the window. From here, I can see part of the driveway where two black SUVs sit idling. Three figures stand at the property line—twin bulky silhouettes I recognize instantly, and a leaner figure between them. All alphas, their aggressive postures visible even at this distance.

Silas strides toward them, shotgun held with casual confidence. Even from here, I can see how his military training has resurfaced—the measured pace, the tactical awareness of cover and sight lines. A warrior protecting his territory.

I crack the window to hear.

"Private property," Silas calls, voice carrying easily across the yard. "Turn around and leave."

One of the Twins—Brady, with the scar across his cheek—steps forward. "We're looking for someone who belongs to us. Omega female, two pups. Our alpha wants them back."

"Nobody here belongs to you." Silas's stance shifts subtly, readying.

"We tracked them to this property," the middle figure says, and my heart stops at the voice—not a hired enforcer, but Daniel himself. "The omega is mine by pack law. The children are my wards. You're harboring runaways."

"They're under my protection now." Silas's voice drops an octave, pure alpha dominance radiating from every syllable. "And you're trespassing."

The scent of competing alphas carries even to where I stand—pine and gunpowder clashing with Daniel's cologne and chemical rage. A territorial dispute with me as the prize.

Daniel laughs, the sound oily and familiar in a way that makes my skin crawl. "You can't claim another alpha's property."

"She was never yours." Silas takes one deliberate step forward. "None of them were. And if you take one more step onto my land, you'll learn exactly what happens to poachers in these mountains."

The threat hangs in the air, deadly serious.

For a moment, I think Daniel might back down. Then he gestures sharply to the Twins. "Bring her out. Kill him if he interferes."

Everything happens at once. The Twins rush forward, Brian drawing a handgun while Brady pulls something that glints in the fading light. Silas moves with terrifying speed, shotgun booming once, twice. Not aiming to kill—I see dirt kick up at their feet—but the warning shots startle them enough for Silas to close the distance.

What follows is brutal efficiency. Silas swings the shotgun like a club, catching Brian across the jaw with the stock. In the same fluid movement, he drops to avoid Brady's swinging blade, then drives upward with an elbow that connects with crushing force. Both Twins stagger, but they're trained fighters too. They circle, regrouping.

Daniel hangs back, shouting orders, his face contorted with rage.

I should stay put. I should trust Silas. But the gun in my hand feels like a responsibility, and the children—my siblings—are somewhere below in a panic room, terrified and alone.

Decision made, I bolt from the bedroom, moving swiftly through the unfamiliar house toward the kitchen. There, a trapdoor stands open in the floor beside the island. I descend the narrow stairs, finding Mia and Liam huddled on a cot in a small, windowless room stocked with supplies.

"Anna!" Liam launches himself at me, trembling arms wrapping around my waist.

"It's Daniel, isn't it?" Mia asks, face pale but determined. "He found us."

"Yes, but Silas is handling it." I check the gun's safety, tuck it into the waistband of my borrowed sweatpants. "Stay here. I need to help him."

"Anna, no—" Mia starts, but I'm already climbing back up the stairs.

"Lock this behind me," I order. "Don't open it for anyone but me or Silas. No matter what you hear."

Outside, the fight has escalated. Silas bleeds from a cut on his shoulder, but both Twins look worse—one limping badly, the other struggling to stand. Daniel paces behind them, shouting something I can't make out.

I slip through shadows toward the barn, intending to circle around behind Daniel. The heat in my blood has receded entirely, replaced by cold fury and determination. These men threatened my family. My alpha. My future.

Before I can get into position, Silas catches sight of me. For a split second, his concentration wavers—not fear for himself, but for me. Brady seizes the opening, lunging with his knife.

Silas twists, but not quite fast enough. The blade slices along his ribs, drawing a fresh line of red. The scent of his blood hits me like a physical blow. Something primal and protective roars to life in my chest.

I raise the gun, aiming not at Brady but at Daniel—the head of the snake.

"Daniel!" I shout. "It's me you want. I'm right here."

All heads turn. Daniel's face contorts with ugly triumph. "Annabelle. Being difficult as always."

"Leave now," I say, voice steadier than I feel. "Or I put a bullet between your eyes."

He smirks. "You won't shoot me. You don't have it in you."

"Try me." I release the safety with an audible click. "You threatened my siblings. You sent men to hunt us. You're on my alpha's property uninvited."

"Your alpha?" Daniel's face darkens with rage. "You're mine. I made you. I sheltered you. I—"

"You never had me." My finger tightens on the trigger. "And you never will."

Something in my expression must convince him, because his bravado falters. He takes a step back, then another.

"The council will hear about this," he spits. "Territorial infringement. Omega theft."

"Let them." Silas has regained his footing, blood streaming down his side but stance steady. "I know the Sheriff in Sanctuary. He'd be real interested in hearing about an alpha forcing himself on an unwilling omega, threatening pre-designation pups."

At the mention of Sanctuary, Daniel's face goes slack with shock. "Sanctuary? This is—"

"The edge of Sanctuary Pack territory," Silas confirms, satisfaction evident. "You know what that means."

I do. Everyone in our world knows. Sanctuary—the rumored haven where pack law protect the vulnerable. Where omegas receive automatic asylum. Where alpha aggression against the unwilling is punished without mercy.

Daniel's face twists with hatred, but calculation replaces his rage. "This isn't over," he snarls, then barks at the Twins: "We're leaving."

"Boss—" Brady begins to protest, but Daniel cuts him off with a vicious gesture.

"Now. Before others come." He backs toward their vehicles, never taking his eyes off us. "She's not worth dying for."

They retreat, dragging their wounded pride and bodies. Silas doesn't lower the shotgun until their taillights disappear down the mountain road.

The adrenaline leaves my body in a rush, knees buckling. Silas is at my side instantly, one arm around my waist, supporting me despite his own injuries.

"The children—" I begin.

"Are safe," he assures me. "I need to secure the perimeter, make sure they're really gone."

I nod, letting him guide me toward the barn. Inside, he sets me on a hay bale, then moves efficiently around the space, checking doors and windows, making a quick call to someone named Jake about "unwelcome visitors headed east on the county road."

Blood still seeps from the cut on his ribs. When he returns to my side, I reach for him, fingers tracing the edge of the wound. "You're hurt."

"Surface cut." He catches my hand, brings it to his lips. "What were you thinking, coming out like that? They could have taken you."

"They were hurting you." The simplicity of it surprises even me. "I couldn't stay hidden while you fought my battles."

Something changes in his expression—respect mingling with the protective instinct. "You're not what I expected, Annabelle."

"Neither are you." My fingers spread across his bare chest, feeling the thundering of his heart. "Thank you for protecting us."

"Always will." His voice roughens, pupils dilating as he inhales deeply. "Your heat—"

"Coming back," I confirm, already feeling the familiar warmth building low in my belly. The danger, the adrenaline, the sight of my alpha defending us—it's accelerated the cycle. "The children?"

"Safe in the panic room for now." His hands slide down my sides, possessive. "Need to check the property first. Make sure they're really gone."

But his body says otherwise—hard muscle pressing against me, the scent of his rut intensifying in response to my rising heat. The alpha who protected his territory now needs to claim his mate.

I rise on tiptoes, nipping at his lower lip. "Check me first."

Whatever restraint he's been clinging to shatters. He backs me against the barn wall, mouth claiming mine in a kiss that's all teeth and tongue and primal possession. My body responds instantly, slick dampening my thighs as he lifts me, wrapping my legs around his waist.

"Mine," he growls against my throat. "Say it again."

"Yours," I gasp as his hand slides beneath the borrowed shirt, finding me bare and ready. "Only yours."

Clothes are shoved aside with desperate urgency. He enters me in one powerful thrust that punches the air from my lungs. There's nothing gentle about this coupling—it's raw, animalistic claim-staking. Each drive of his hips slams my back against the rough wood, pain and pleasure blurring into pure sensation.

"Never—" thrust "—letting—" thrust "—anyone—" thrust "—take you." His voice is barely human, alpha instincts in full control.

I cling to his shoulders, nails drawing fresh lines of red across battle-marked skin. "No one could," I promise between gasps. "Only want you. Only ever you."

His knot swells faster this time, stretching me almost past endurance before locking us together. The slight pain tips me over the edge, orgasm crashing through me in waves that leave me sobbing his name. He follows immediately, teeth finding my neck in what could easily become a mating bite if he pressed harder.

He doesn't. Even in this feral state, he respects my choice.

The realization breaks something open inside me—trust flowering in soil I thought permanently salted. I turn my head, offering better access to my neck, silently granting permission.

Silas freezes, understanding the gesture's significance. "Annabelle," he breathes against my skin, question and reverence in that single word.

"Yes," I whisper, certain in a way I've never been. "Make me yours, Silas. Completely."

His teeth sink into the gland at my neck, breaking skin, exchanging the biochemical signature that will mark me as his mate for life. Pain flares bright, then transforms into pleasure so intense my vision whites out. I feel him pulsing inside me, his release triggered by the mating bond forming between us.

When awareness returns, we're still joined, his forehead resting against mine as we breathe each other's air. Blood—his and mine—mingles on our skin, but neither of us moves to clean it.

"Mine," he says again, but differently now. Less possessive, more wondering.

I touch the mark at my neck, still tender but already healing. "Yours," I confirm. "And you're mine."

His smile—the first real one I've seen—transforms his face from forbidding to breathtaking. "Damn right I am."

8

D awn breaks with painful clarity, casting harsh light on decisions made in darkness. I wake slowly, cataloging sensations: sheets tangled around bare legs, the pleasant ache between my thighs, the throb of the fresh mating mark at my neck. Silas sleeps beside me, one heavy arm draped possessively across my waist, his breathing deep and even. His face in repose looks younger, the hard lines of vigilance softened by sleep. I touch the mark he left on me, the raised edges of the bite tender under my fingertips. What have I done? Heat-decisions rarely survive the cold light of morning. I've tied myself—tied all of us—to a man I've known for mere weeks, driven by biology and fear rather than reason. Yet as I watch his chest rise and fall, scent our mingled pheromones saturating the sheets, I can't bring myself to regret it. What terrifies me isn't the bond itself but the possibility that he might.

I ease from beneath his arm, wincing as various muscles protest yesterday's activities. The bite at my neck pulses in time with my heartbeat, still fresh enough that the bond feels like a live wire connecting us. His shirt—the one I grabbed in haste when Daniel arrived—still hangs from my frame, smelling of both of us now.

In the adjoining bathroom, I stare at my reflection, taking inventory. My neck bears not just the mating bite but a constellation of smaller marks—evidence of Silas's possessive passion. My lips are swollen, hair a tangled mess. I look claimed. Thoroughly. Permanently.

But what happens now?

Heat may have driven us together, biology cementing the attraction, but life isn't just biology. It's practicalities. Three extra mouths to feed. Two children to raise. A past that might still come hunting us despite Daniel's retreat.

Are we a burden Silas will come to resent?

I shower quickly, borrowing his soap, oddly comforted by the way it mixes with my natural scent. When I emerge, wrapped in his robe, the bed is empty. Voices drift from elsewhere in the house—Liam's excited chatter, Mia's more measured tones, Silas's deep rumble answering them.

I follow the sounds to the kitchen, pausing in the doorway to observe unnoticed.

Silas stands at the stove, competently flipping pancakes while explaining something about cattle rotation to a fascinated Liam. The boy perches on a counter stool, hanging on every word, occasionally asking questions that reveal how closely he's listening. Mia sets the table with easy familiarity, moving around Silas's kitchen like she's done it a hundred times.

They look like a family. Not guests or refugees, but people who belong here.

"Anna!" Liam spots me first, face lighting up. "Silas is teaching me about winter cattle management!"

Silas turns, spatula in hand, and the look that crosses his face steals my breath—pure, unguarded joy mingled with possessive satisfaction. His eyes linger on the collar of the robe where it covers his mark, and his scent spikes with alpha pride.

"Morning," he says, voice rough around the edges. "Hungry?"

The double meaning isn't lost on either of us. My cheeks heat, but I manage a nod. "Starving, actually."

Mia's eyes dart between us, missing nothing. At fourteen, she's old enough to understand the significance of what's happened. "You guys mated," she says bluntly.

Liam's eyes widen. "For real? Like, forever-mated?"

I cross to the coffee pot, buying time.

"Yes," I finally say. "We did."

"Does that mean we're staying?" Liam's question cuts straight to the heart of it.

I look to Silas, suddenly uncertain.

"This is your home now," he answers without hesitation. "All of you. If that's what you want."

"We can't just—" I begin.

"Yes, we can," Mia interrupts, surprising me. She sets down the last fork with deliberate precision. "Anna, we've been running for months. We're exhausted. You're exhausted." Her young face is serious beyond her years. "And you mated him. That's not something you'd do if you didn't feel safe here."

My throat tightens. "It's not that simple. There are practicalities—"

"Like what?" Silas slides the last pancake onto a platter, turns off the burner. "School for the kids? Already called the principal at Sanctuary Elementary. They can start after Thanksgiving break."

I blink. "You what?"

"Made calls this morning while you were showering." He meets my gaze steadily. "Also talked to Jake—he's the Sheriff. He's putting the word out about Daniel. Any alpha who tries to claim a mated omega faces serious charges in Sanctuary territory."

"You've been busy," I manage, overwhelmed by his efficiency.

He shrugs, but there's nothing casual about the intensity in his eyes. "You're my mate now. The kids are pack. Making sure you're all settled isn't a favor—it's my responsibility. My privilege."

After breakfast, Silas takes us on what he calls "the official tour" of the ranch—not as guests this time, but as family. He shows Liam the workshop where he plans to teach him more woodworking. He discusses chicken breeding programs with Mia, treating her ideas with genuine respect. And for me, he outlines the business side of the operation, areas where my organizational skills could complement his practical knowledge.

"The east pasture needs work," he says as we stand overlooking rolling hills. "Been thinking about subdividing it, rotating crops instead of just grazing. Could use someone with a good head for numbers to make it profitable."

"Is that me?" I ask, caught between amusement and something deeper.

"You managed to keep two kids alive and moving across three states with minimal resources." His hand finds mine, fingers intertwining. "I'd say you're pretty damn capable."

Later, he takes me to a small office in the back of the house. Spread across the desk are papers—property maps, bank statements, legal documents.

"What's all this?" I ask.

"Adding your name." He indicates a stack of forms. "Joint ownership. The land, the house, the accounts. Everything."

I stare at him, speechless.

"Mating isn't just biology," he says, reading my earlier thoughts with uncanny accuracy. "It's a partnership. I want you to feel secure. To know that what's mine is yours—legally, not just in words."

"Silas, this is too much—"

"It's not enough." He steps closer, one hand lifting to trace the edge of his mark on my neck. "I've been alone a long time, Annabelle. Built all this with no one to share it with. Now I have you. The kids. A family." His voice roughens. "Don't tell me it's too much when it's everything I never knew I needed."

Something breaks open inside me—a dam holding back hope, holding back trust. I lean into his touch, letting myself believe that this impossible thing might be real after all.

"I'm scared," I admit, the words barely audible.

"Of what?"

"That it's too good to be true. That I'll wake up and be back in Daniel's compound, or running with the kids, or—"

He silences me with a kiss, gentle but thorough. "This is real," he murmurs against my lips. "We're real. And nobody's taking you from me."

That evening, we sit on the porch swing, watching the kids explore their new territory with the uninhibited joy of the young. Mia charts the chicken coop expansion on graph paper. Liam races around the paddock, naming each cow he encounters.

"They've never had this," I say softly. "Space. Freedom. Safety."

Silas's arm tightens around my shoulders. "Neither have you."

He's right. I've been running so long—first within Daniel's compound, finding ways to avoid his attention, then physically running across state lines. Always looking over my shoulder, always waiting for the other shoe to drop.

"It's hard to believe we can just... stop," I confess. "Build a life here. Be normal."

"Not normal," he corrects, pressing a kiss to my temple. "Extraordinary. A family forged in fire." His hand covers mine, resting on my still-flat stomach. "Maybe growing, someday, when you're ready."

The thought of carrying Silas's pup—a child born of choice and love rather than coercion—sends a rush of warmth through me that has nothing to do with heat biology.

"I'd like that," I whisper, surprising myself with the truth of it. "Someday."

His smile against my skin feels like a promise. As the sun sets over Hawthorne Ranch—our ranch now—I let myself imagine a future measured not in escapes and hiding places, but in seasons and harvests, birthdays and anniversaries.

For the first time since my parents died, home feels like more than a word.

9

The cruiser appears on our driveway just after noon, kicking up dust that catches golden in the November sun. I freeze at the kitchen window, dishcloth clutched in suddenly bloodless fingers. Official vehicles still trigger my flight response—too many close calls, too many corrupt officials in Daniel's pocket. Silas materializes beside me, his hand settling warm and steady at the small of my back.

"That's Jake," he says, reading my tension. "Sheriff Rawlins. He's pack, not threat."

I force myself to breathe as the vehicle stops and two men emerge—one in tan uniform with a star on his chest, the other in firefighter's pants and a department t-shirt stretched across broad shoulders. Both alphas, but their scent lacks the aggressive edge I've come to expect. The Sheriff tips his hat back, squinting up at the house.

"Well, I'll be damned," he calls out. "Silas Hawthorne, finally took a mate. Hell must've frozen solid overnight."

Silas's chest rumbles with what might be a chuckle. "Come meet them," he murmurs, steering me gently toward the door. I resist the urge to check my appearance—the mating mark visible above my shirt collar, my hair hastily pulled back, wearing borrowed jeans rolled at the ankles because nothing here fits me quite right.

Outside, Silas's posture shifts subtly—still protective, but with the ease of long friendship. "Jake," he nods to the Sheriff. "Ethan," to the firefighter. "This is Annabelle. My mate."

The pride in his voice sends warmth cascading through me.

Sheriff Rawlins—Jake—steps forward, respectfully keeping enough distance not to crowd a newly mated omega. He's older than Silas, silver threading his dark hair, laugh lines etched deep around keen eyes. "Pleasure to meet you, Annabelle. Welcome to Sanctuary."

The firefighter—Ethan—grins, dimples creasing his cheeks. Younger, maybe early thirties, with an open face that suggests easy humor.

"Never thought I'd see the day this grumpy bastard found someone willing to put up with him," he teases, earning a mock growl from Silas.

"We picked up three of Daniel Prescott's men on the edge of town last night," Jake says, tone shifting to business. "Banged up pretty good. Said they had car trouble, but the scent of your property was all over them."

Silas's arm tightens around my waist. "They came looking for Annabelle and her siblings. I sent them packing."

"Figured as much." Jake nods. "I've put out alerts to neighboring jurisdictions. Prescott's pack has a reputation—not a good one. They won't find friendly reception if they try to come back."

"What about pack law?" I ask, finally finding my voice. "Daniel claimed I belonged to him. That the children were his wards."

Jake's expression hardens. "Pack law's different in Sanctuary territory, ma'am. No alpha can claim an unwilling omega here, regardless of prior arrangements. And minors can't be forced into pack bonds they don't consent to." He gestures to my neck where Silas's mark sits. "Besides, you're mated now. Even traditional packs respect that bond."

"We came to make it official," Ethan adds, pulling paperwork from his back pocket. "Sanctuary Pack protection declaration. You, your siblings, and your property fall under our jurisdiction now. Any attempt to remove you or harm you is considered an act of aggression against the entire pack."

I stare at the documents he extends, unable to believe it could be that simple. After months of running, of looking over our shoulders, of sleeping in shifts—protection offered freely, without conditions or collateral.

"Is this real?" I whisper, more to myself than them.

Jake's weathered face softens. "As real as it gets, ma'am. This town was founded as a haven. It's what we do."

"Anna!" Liam's voice breaks the moment as he races around the corner of the house, Mia following at a more dignified pace. "There's a police car! Are we in trouble?"

Jake crouches to Liam's level, his large frame somehow becoming less intimidating. "No trouble at all, young man. I'm Sheriff Rawlins. Just making sure you and your family are settled in proper."

Liam studies him with the frank curiosity of childhood. "Do you have a gun?"

"Liam," I begin, mortified, but Jake just laughs.

"I do indeed. Part of the job. You must be Liam, and this is Mia?" He nods to my sister, who hangs back slightly, inherent alpha caution making her reserved around these new pack members.

"You know our names?" she asks, suspicion coloring her voice.

"Silas called me this morning. Said we had new pack members who needed looking after." Jake straightens, addressing both children with respectful seriousness. "In Sanctuary, we take care of our own. You're safe here."

Mia's gaze flicks from Jake to Ethan to me, measuring. "What about school? Our records are still with our old pack."

"Already handled," Ethan pipes up. "My mate works in the school office. New student enrollment doesn't require previous records in special circumstances." He winks at her. "Special circumstances being you're under Sanctuary protection now."

I watch as the children absorb this information—Liam with immediate trust, Mia with cautious hope. Their entire lives have been defined by Daniel's control, by the precarious safety of his "protection" that came with so many strings attached. Freedom is a foreign concept.

"Why don't you two show Ethan your chicken operation?" Silas suggests. "He's got some experience with livestock himself."

As they lead the firefighter toward the coop, Jake turns to us with a more serious expression. "Daniel Prescott has influence in certain counties," he says quietly. "But not here. Sanctuary was established over a hundred years ago as neutral territory—a place where pack politics don't override basic rights."

"I've heard rumors," I admit. "Never believed they were true."

"Most don't, until they need us," Jake says simply. "Town looks ordinary enough, but we've got a system. Everyone watches out for everyone else, especially newcomers who might need… special consideration."

"Like runaway omegas?" I can't keep the bitterness from my voice.

"Like anyone who needs a second chance," he corrects gently. "We don't ask questions about where folks came from. Only care about where they're going."

After the paperwork is signed and the men depart—not before extracting promises to attend the upcoming Thanksgiving potluck at the firehouse—Silas suggests we drive into town. "You should see Sanctuary properly," he says. "Not just hear about it."

The town itself is picture-perfect small-town America—one main street lined with storefronts, a diner on the corner, a small park at the center. But as we drive slowly through, Silas points out details I'd miss otherwise.

"Marge's Place—best breakfast in three counties. Marge hires omegas, no questions asked. Safe place for newcomers to land." He nods toward the cheerful diner. "The motel at the edge of town—owner's an omega who escaped an arranged mating thirty years ago. He keeps two rooms permanently reserved for emergency cases."

We pass a school, a small medical clinic, a community center. At each, Silas mentions some aspect of their unspoken mission—the teacher who specializes in helping traumatized children, the doctor who treats injuries without reporting to authorities, the community events designed to integrate newcomers.

"It's like an underground railroad," I murmur, watching ordinary-looking people go about their business. "Hidden in plain sight."

"That's exactly what it is," Silas confirms, pride evident. "Most folks who settle here have their own stories. Their own reasons for valuing sanctuary."

"Including you?" I ask, studying his profile.

His hands tighten slightly on the steering wheel. "Marines taught me to protect. Coming home, finding this place—it gave that instinct purpose."

We stop at the general store, where Silas introduces me to the beta couple who own it. They welcome me without prying questions, their genuine warmth evident in the care they take helping me select clothes and essentials for the children and myself.

"Put it on our account," Silas tells them, ignoring my protests.

"First week's always on the house for newcomers anyway," the woman—Carol—winks at me. "Town tradition."

As we drive home, the car filled with bags, I watch the landscape transform from neat town to wild mountain beauty. Sanctuary spreads below us like a promise kept—ordinary and extraordinary all at once.

"I never thought we'd stop running," I admit quietly. "Even after we found you, I kept waiting for the other shoe to drop. For someone to demand payment for safety."

Silas reaches across the console, taking my hand in his. "The only payment Sanctuary asks is that you do the same for others someday. Pass it forward."

I think of other omegas still trapped, other children living in fear. "I can do that," I promise.

As we crest the hill that reveals Hawthorne Ranch—our ranch—sprawled below, I see Mia and Liam in the yard. They've dragged out old lawn chairs, arranging them in a circle like they're planning a campfire. Planning to stay. To live rather than just survive.

"They belong here," I say softly.

Silas brings my hand to his lips. "So do you."

For the first time, I believe it might be true.

10

Twilight settles over the ranch like a worn quilt, familiar despite our short time here. I sit on the porch steps, watching shadows stretch across land that legal documents now say is partly mine. Inside, Silas helps the children with math homework at the kitchen table, his deep voice patient as he explains fractions to a frustrated Liam. The scene through the window looks like something from someone else's life—domestic, secure, ordinary in the most extraordinary way.

The mating mark on my neck has healed to a silvery scar, no longer painful but still sensitive to touch. Our scents have fully merged, creating something new and uniquely ours. Biology satisfied. But in the quiet moments, when heat and danger aren't driving our decisions, I find myself asking the question I've been too afraid to voice: Is biology enough?

A week has passed since the Sheriff's visit. A week of establishing routines, of gradually moving our belongings from the bunkhouse to the main house, of learning the rhythms of shared space. Silas hasn't pushed for more intimacy beyond what my lingering heat demanded. He's been careful, respectful—almost too much so, as if afraid of spooking me.

I trace patterns in the weathered wood of the porch step, thinking of all the small moments that have accumulated like pebbles in a jar. Silas teaching Mia to drive the tractor, his large hands steady on hers as she navigated the field. The night Liam had a nightmare about Daniel, and Silas sat with him until dawn, telling stories of his own childhood to chase away the shadows. The way he asks my opinion on ranch decisions, genuinely valuing my input. How he leaves coffee ready for me every morning, remembering exactly how I take it after being told just once.

None of these things have anything to do with being mates. None are driven by biology or obligation. They're choices—daily, deliberate choices to care, to see us, to make space for us in his life.

The screen door creaks, and I know without looking that it's him. His scent—our scent now—wraps around me as he settles beside me on the step, not touching but close enough that I feel his warmth.

"Kids are doing their reading," he says. "Liam finally figured out those fractions."

I smile. "He's smart. Just needs confidence."

"Like his sister." His voice holds quiet pride, as if the children's accomplishments are his own. In a way, I suppose they are becoming so.

We sit in companionable silence, watching the first stars appear.

"Penny for your thoughts," he finally says. "You've been quiet today."

I consider deflecting, offering some trivial observation about ranch work or the children. But that's the old Annabelle—the one who survived by hiding, by keeping parts of herself locked away where they couldn't be used against her.

"I'm thinking about choice," I say instead. "About fate versus free will."

He turns slightly, giving me his full attention. "Heavy thoughts for a Tuesday."

"We mated during my heat," I continue, watching his face carefully. "Biology pushed us together. Danger cemented it. But now that those pressures are gone..."

"You're wondering if it was real." No accusation in his voice, just understanding.

"I'm wondering if it's enough," I correct gently. "If biology is enough to build a life on."

He's quiet for so long I think perhaps he won't answer. When he does, his voice has roughened with emotion.

"My parents were a biological match," he says. "Perfect compatibility on paper. Miserable in reality. He was cruel, she was bitter. They stayed together because biology told them to, even though they made each other's lives hell." His hand finds mine on the porch step, fingers interlacing. "Biology's just the starting point, Annabelle. The map, not the journey."

"And what is our journey?" I ask, heart in my throat.

"Whatever we choose to make it." His thumb traces circles on my wrist. "The mating happened fast. I don't regret it—couldn't regret it if I tried—but I understand if you need time to be sure."

"That's not—" I turn to face him fully. "Silas, I'm not unsure about you."

Confusion crosses his face. "Then what—"

"I'm unsure about me." The admission costs me, but it feels right to voice it. "About what I have to offer. You've given us so much—safety, security, a home. What do I bring to this bond besides three mouths to feed and a complicated past?"

Understanding dawns in his eyes, followed by something fiercer. "Is that what you think? That this is some kind of... charity arrangement?"

I shrug, uncomfortable with his intensity. "You're a good man who saw people in need. It's natural to want to help."

"Bullshit." The word cracks between us, sharp and unexpected. "You think I mated you out of pity? Out of some misguided savior complex?"

"I think you mated me because biology said we were compatible and circumstances pushed us together," I answer honestly. "And I think you're kind enough, honorable enough, to stand by that decision regardless."

He rises abruptly, pacing the length of the porch. When he turns back, his expression is raw, exposed in a way I've never seen before.

"I mated you because from the moment you showed up on my property—soaking wet, exhausted, still standing between danger and those kids like nothing could make you move—I haven't been able to think straight." The words pour out of him, unfiltered. "I mated you because you're the strongest person I've ever met. Because you call me on my shit. Because you see the world clearer than anyone I know."

He kneels before me, taking both my hands in his.

"I mated you because this place—this life I built—was hollow until you three filled it. Because Liam's laugh makes everything brighter. Because Mia's determination reminds me what courage looks like. Because your smile is the first thing I want to see every morning for the rest of my life."

Tears blur my vision, but I don't look away.

"The mate pull just showed me what I would have eventually figured out on my own," he continues, voice gentling. "That you're it for me, Annabelle. Biology or no biology. And if you need time to feel the same way, I'll wait."

I stare at this man—this alpha who asks instead of demands, who sees strength where others have only ever seen submission value, who talks about waiting when biology says he could claim.

And suddenly, the decision I've been circling becomes blindingly clear.

I reach out, tracing the line of his jaw with trembling fingers. "I don't need time," I whisper. "I just needed to know this was real for you too. That it wasn't just biology or circumstance or obligation."

"It's real." He turns his face to press a kiss to my palm. "Realer than anything I've ever known."

"Then I choose you, Silas Hawthorne." I lean forward until our foreheads touch. "Not because fate said so, or because you saved us, or because we mated during my heat. I choose you because of who you are. Because I love you."

The words—ones I've never said to any alpha—hang in the air between us. For a moment, he goes utterly still. Then a smile breaks across his face, transforming it completely.

"Say that again," he breathes.

"I love you." Easier the second time, like my heart recognizes the truth of it.

He gathers me against him, burying his face in my neck, inhaling our combined scent at the mating mark. "I love you too," he murmurs against my skin. "Have since that first night, I think. Just didn't know what to call it then."

Later, after the children are asleep, we sit at the kitchen table, making plans that have nothing to do with necessity and everything to do with choice. School programs for Mia and Liam. Expansion of the garden come spring. Converting the old study into a proper room for Liam, with space for his growing collection of carved animals.

"I want to work with Sanctuary's support network," I tell him. "Help other omegas who come through. Pay it forward, like you said."

He nods, unsurprised. "You'd be good at that. You understand what they need."

"And I want more for us," I add quietly. "Not right away, but... someday. When we're ready."

His eyes darken with understanding. "Pups."

"A family that's ours together. A new branch on the tree, not just grafted parts."

He reaches across the table, hand covering mine. "I'd like that. Very much."

We talk late into the night, painting our future in broad strokes and fine details. Not fate's design, but our own. Not biology's imperative, but hearts' desire.

A chosen path. A shared journey. A love that transcends instinct to become something far more powerful—conscious, deliberate, freely given.

11

—·—

Moonlight spills through the bedroom window, painting silver streaks across the floorboards. The house creaks and settles around us, a living thing adjusting to new inhabitants. Down the hall, Mia and Liam sleep soundly, their scents content and peaceful in a way they haven't been since before our parents died.

Silas moves behind me, his chest warm against my back as we stand at the window, watching night claim the land that's become our sanctuary in every sense of the word. His arms circle my waist, lips brushing the mating mark at my neck—a touch so gentle it makes my breath catch.

"The children are asleep," he murmurs, the rumble of his voice vibrating against my skin. "We have the night to ourselves."

Unlike our first frantic coupling driven by heat and rut, unlike our second claiming born of adrenaline and danger, this moment unfolds slowly, deliberately. A choice we're making with clear eyes and full hearts.

I turn in his arms, tracing the strong line of his jaw with my fingertips. "No biology pushing us this time," I say softly. "No emergency. Just us."

His eyes—storm-cloud gray in daylight, almost black in the moonlit room—hold mine with an intensity that still steals my breath.

"Just us," he echoes, voice rough with emotion rather than lust. "The way it should be."

When he kisses me, it's different from before—unhurried, exploratory, as if we have all the time in the world. Which, I realize with a rush of joy, we do. This isn't stolen pleasure between crises. This is the beginning of our life together.

His hands move reverently over my body, not claiming but cherishing. I respond in kind, mapping the terrain of scars and muscle that tell the story of the man he's become. We undress each other slowly, each newly revealed inch of skin acknowledged with touches, kisses, whispered appreciations.

"You're beautiful," he breathes against my collarbone, and for the first time in my life, I believe it—not because of how I look, but because of how he sees me.

When he lifts me onto the bed, the sheets are cool against my heated skin. He follows, covering my body with his larger frame, but there's nothing overwhelming about his presence now. He holds himself above me, careful not to crush, attentive to every response.

"I want to memorize you," he says, trailing kisses down my sternum. "Every freckle. Every scar. Every place that makes you gasp."

He does exactly as he promised—his hands, his mouth, his very soul moving over me with a level of care I never believed an alpha capable of. He learns my body's every secret, and not as a conqueror mapping new territory, but as a craftsman learning the grain of a beloved piece of wood, the knots and whorls and fragile veins. He finds the sensitive spot behind my ear that makes me shiver, then returns to it again and again, marveling at the helpless tremor he can draw from me with the brush of his lips. He seeks the ticklish hollow of my knee and, when I laugh, he looks at me as if I've just performed magic. He traces the bone of my ankle, the curve of my hip, the scar from the night I lost everything, and he never once asks for more than I'm willing to give. He asks with every touch, and listens to every answer my body gives.

I return the favor, hungry to know everything about him. I count the scars on his body and ask the story behind each one. Some he tells—shrapnel from a hunting accident as a boy, an angry barn cat defending her litter, a jagged line left by barbed wire during a flood rescue before he ever knew my name. Each history anchors him further in the present, in me. I trace the outline of the ancient tattoo on his ribs, black and blue fire curling around the names of fallen brothers-in-arms, and kiss each letter in reverence for what he has lost. There is a spot just beneath his jaw, a tender valley that makes his breath catch when I press my lips there, and when he hisses and tilts his head to give me better access I feel a surge of power unlike any I've ever known.

His hand slides up my thigh, pausing at the crease of my hip. I press into his touch, and only then does he continue upward. I trace the ridge of his collarbone with my fingertips. He shivers, then mirrors the gesture along my ribs. When I gasp and arch against him, his eyes widen, pupils dilating. The corner of his mouth lifts in that crooked smile, and he dips his head to follow the path his fingers blazed. I thread my fingers through his hair, tugging gently, and he looks up at me with parted lips, a flush spreading across his cheeks as if my touch is a gift he never expected to

The first time he slides into me, it's not a collision or a claiming. It's a slow, deliberate joining—his body sheathing mine with a patience that borders on reverence. He rests his forehead against mine, and for a long moment, neither of us moves. Our breathing synchronizes, the thrum of my heart echoing in his chest where it presses against mine. I feel open and vulnerable in a way that terrifies me, and yet—even more terrifying—I want this vulnerability. I crave it. I crave him.

"Are you okay?" he whispers, voice roughened with restraint.

"I want you," I say, and the words feel not like surrender but like a vow.

He grins, the crooked smile that never fails to undo me, and begins to move. The rhythm is maddeningly slow, his control absolute; every withdrawal is followed by a deeper return, as if he's determined to anchor himself inside me with every stroke. My body responds eagerly, matching him movement for movement, need spiraling higher but never frantic. Not this time. This time, we are building something, not burning it down.

He keeps his eyes on mine, refusing to look away even when sensation threatens to overwhelm. It feels like a dare. It feels like a promise. He brushes his thumb along my cheekbone, grounding me, and I realize I am not clinging to him for safety—I am holding him because I want to, because this physical bond is the expression of something truer and deeper than biology.

"I love you," I whisper, the words still new enough to taste miraculous on my tongue.

His rhythm falters, emotion overwhelming physical need for a moment.

"Say it again," he asks, as he did on the porch.

"I love you, Silas Hawthorne." I cup his face in my hands, making sure he sees the truth in my eyes. "Not because fate decided it. Because I do."

Something breaks open in his expression—the last wall crumbling, the final guard lowered. He kisses me deeply, his movements becoming more urgent, though no less tender.

"You're everything," he murmurs against my lips. "Everything I never dared hope for."

When his knot begins to swell, stretching me from within, it feels like the physical manifestation of a promise we've already made. He watches my face carefully, even now mindful of my comfort.

"Yes," I breathe, urging him deeper. "Complete the bond. Make me yours again."

With one final, gentle thrust, his knot locks us together, triggering my release. I cry out his name, back arching as pleasure washes through me in waves. He follows immediately, his larger frame trembling as he empties himself deep inside me.

In the aftermath, we lie tangled together, his weight a comfort rather than a burden, his heartbeat a steady rhythm against my chest. The mating mark on my neck pulses in time with our joined heartbeats, the bond between us humming with renewed strength.

"Different this time," he murmurs, brushing damp hair from my forehead.

I nod, understanding exactly what he means. "Better."

"Not better," he corrects gently. "Just… more complete. This wasn't heat or rut or danger. Just us, choosing each other."

"I'll keep choosing you," I promise. "Every day."

His smile—still rare enough to feel like a gift—warms me from within. "And I'll spend the rest of my life making sure you never regret it."

We stay joined until his knot subsides, neither of us willing to break the connection before we must. When we finally separate, he doesn't move away, instead gathering me against his side, my head pillowed on his chest.

"First time I saw this place," he says quietly, "I knew it could be something special. Somewhere I could build a life that made sense after what I'd seen overseas." His fingers trace idle patterns on my bare shoulder. "But it wasn't complete until you three arrived."

I think of the ranch as it was when we first stumbled up that muddy drive—imposing, beautiful, but somehow empty despite its grandeur. And how it feels now—warm with life and purpose, echoing with Liam's laughter and Mia's determined footsteps.

"We needed this place," I acknowledge. "But maybe it needed us too."

"No maybe about it," he says with certainty. "Land needs people who love it. A house needs a family to become a home."

Family. The word settles around us like a blessing. Not just biology or legality, but choice and commitment and love. We fall asleep tangled together, the moon our witness, the future unspooling before us like the land beyond our window—vast with possibility.

Spring arrives in a riot of wildflowers, painting the meadows with colors so vibrant they almost hurt to look at after winter's monochrome palette. Six months have transformed Hawthorne Ranch from a refuge to a home, from a stopping place to the center of our world.

Mia thrives in Sanctuary's school system, her natural alpha tendencies finding positive outlets in leadership roles and competitive sports. At fifteen, she's already talking about agricultural college, about modernizing parts of the ranch operation. Silas listens to her ideas with genuine interest, treating her not as a child but as a future partner in the business.

Liam has blossomed from a nervous, silent boy into one who chatters incessantly about his friends, his projects, his growing menagerie of animals both carved and real. The scars Daniel left on him—physical and emotional—haven't disappeared entirely, but they've faded enough that he can go days without flinching at sudden movements, without nightmares jerking him awake.

As for me, I've found purpose beyond survival. The garden has become my domain, expanding from simple vegetable plots to an experiment in sustainable farming practices. Three days a week, I drive into town to work with Sanctuary's support network, helping newly arrived omegas navigate their fresh start.

And Silas... my mate has softened in ways I never expected. The hard edges remain—the vigilance, the protective instincts, the capacity for necessary violence—but they're balanced now by moments of startling tenderness. The man who once lived in self-imposed isolation now hosts community barbecues, coaches Liam's baseball team, sits patiently through Mia's endless chicken breeding presentations.

"Never thought I'd see Hawthorne smiling," Sheriff Jake commented last week at the Founder's Day festival. "Used to worry he'd turn into a hermit up here, nothing but ghosts for company."

"He had ghosts," I agreed, watching Silas lift a giggling Liam onto his shoulders. "But they're quieter now."

Tonight, as summer approaches, we sit on the porch swing after dinner, watching Mia demonstrate her latest training technique with the chickens while Liam provides enthusiastic commentary.

"You know what I was thinking?" Silas says, his arm warm around my shoulders.

"Hmm?"

"The east bedroom—the one we've been using for storage. It would make a good nursery."

My heart stutters, then races. My hand moves unconsciously to my stomach, still flat but perhaps not for much longer. I haven't said anything yet, wanting to be certain before sharing the news that my cycle is late, that my scent has shifted subtly.

"You know," I whisper.

He smiles, pressing a kiss to my temple. "Suspected. Your scent changed about a week ago. Been waiting for you to say something."

"I wanted to be sure." I turn to face him fully. "Are you... is this okay? So soon?"

His hand covers mine where it rests on my abdomen, his expression so nakedly joyful it brings tears to my eyes. "More than okay," he says. "Perfect timing."

As twilight deepens around us, Mia and Liam race each other to the paddock for one last goodnight to the horses. The land stretches peaceful and protected in all directions. Silas's heartbeat remains steady beneath my ear, his scent mingling with mine in the cooling evening air.

This, I realize, is what coming home feels like. Not a place, but a certainty. Not walls and a roof, but arms that hold you close and a bond that anchors your soul.

"I love you," Silas murmurs into my hair.

Simple words. Profound truth.

"I love you too," I answer, and feel the last of my walls crumble completely.

Find out what happens next in Sanctuary with Finn and Jenny's story in The Alpha Deputy! (Continue to the next page for a Bonus Epilogue.)

Want more of Silas and Annabelle? Sign up for the Ash Jade newsletter and download a free bonus scene today! Click here: The Alpha Rancher Bonus Scene

Bonus Epilogue

Finn

I kill the engine but leave the patrol car running. The heater keeps the December chill at bay while I scan the elementary school's perimeter fence, looking for any sign of the "creepy guy" Mrs. Atkins reported seeing on her morning walk. Nothing moves except naked tree branches scratching at a pewter sky. The radio crackles, dispatch asking for an update, but I let it wait. Something feels off—a hunch crawling up my spine that has nothing to do with the approaching winter storm.

Sanctuary Elementary sits like a squat fortress at the edge of town, brick walls and bright plastic playground equipment a stark contrast to the pine-covered mountains that loom behind it. I've been driving past it five times a day since the first report came in three days ago. Nothing but paw prints from the neighbor's retriever and footprints from kids who cut across the field after school.

But today feels different.

I push the car door open, hit by a blast of mountain air that smells of pine and approaching snow. My breath clouds in front of me as I circle the patrol car and head toward the fence line. The grass is dead, winter-brown and crunching under my boots.

"Deputy Calloway checking the school perimeter," I finally respond to dispatch. "No immediate signs of disturbance."

That's not entirely true. As I approach the southeastern corner where the playground meets the tree line, I see it—trampled grass in a pattern too deliberate for wildlife. Someone stood here, watching. The fence hasn't been cut, but there are scuff marks on the metal posts, like someone tested its strength.

I crouch down, tracing the indentation with gloved fingers. An adult-sized shoe print, partially obscured. My jaw tightens.

Something red catches my eye—a small mitten with a cartoon reindeer face, dropped and forgotten. I pick it up, turning it over in my hand. Too small for the shoe print owner. A child's mitten. Might be nothing—kids lose shit all the time—but it sits wrong in my gut.

I bring the mitten to my nose without thinking, an old instinct from my tracking days with the forest service. Beyond the wool and laundry detergent, there's the expected scent of child—innocent, unmarked. But there's something else—a trace of something sharp and unfamiliar that doesn't belong.

My nose wrinkles as I pocket the mitten. I'll drop it at the lost and found later, but for now, it's evidence of… something. I'm not sure what.

I continue along the fence line, eyes scanning the ground. The trampled grass follows the fence for about twenty yards, then stops abruptly at a cluster of pine trees. Whoever was here knew the sight lines, knew where they could stand without being spotted from the school windows.

"You got eyes on anything, Finn?" The radio crackles with Sheriff Jake's voice, gruffer than usual.

"Negative," I respond, keeping it professional despite the unease rippling through me. "But someone was definitely here. Scent trail's wrong. Need to talk to you when I get back."

I don't elaborate over the open channel. In Sanctuary, we're careful about what we say. Too many ears listening, too many packs with their own agendas. Ever since Jake established this town as omega-friendly territory, we've had our share of uninvited visitors with bad intentions.

I make my way back to the car, pulling out my phone to document the trampled areas and fence marks. Not enough to file a formal report, but enough to justify increasing patrols. Enough to justify the growl building in my chest.

This is a school. Full of kids. There are lines you don't cross in my town.

I'm punching in a text to the rest of the deputy team when movement near the side entrance of the school catches my eye. A woman I don't recognize—slender, bundled in a puffy blue coat—is unlocking the door. Her dark hair falls in waves down her back, and even from this distance, I can see the mist of her breath as she hums to herself, keys jingling in her hands.

Something pulls in my chest—sharp and unexpected. I freeze, thumb hovering over my phone screen.

She must sense my stare because she turns, eyes finding mine across the parking lot. For a split second, something electric passes between us. Curiosity flickers across her face, replaced quickly by wariness when she spots my uniform, the patrol car.

But it's her scent that hits me a moment later when the wind shifts—soft, warm, distinctly omega. It drifts across the lot like a question, wrapping around me before I can defend against it. My shoulders drop a fraction, tension bleeding out before I can stop it. Something primal and possessive uncurls in my chest.

I growl low in my throat and look away, breaking whatever the hell that was. Not why I'm here. Not my business. Not my omega.

She's still watching me when I slide back into the patrol car, her head tilted slightly. I catch her gaze again in the rearview mirror as I pull away, driving too fast for a school zone.

"Fuck," I mutter, rolling down the window despite the cold. I need to clear my head, clear my senses of that scent before it takes root. Something about it is too... right. Too perfect. The kind of scent that makes alphas do stupid, territorial things.

The kind of scent that makes me think of den and home and mine—thoughts I have no right to.

I'm halfway back to the station when I realize I never saw her before. Must be new. Sanctuary's small enough that I know most of the staff at the elementary school—or at least, I've seen them around. The principal's an old buddy of Jake's, stern but fair. The secretary's been there since I was a kid. But this woman? Never seen her.

New people in Sanctuary always put me on edge. Half the time they're running from something—or someone. The other half, they're here looking for trouble.

I swing the patrol car into my spot behind the station, engine ticking as it cools. The building's not much—converted from an old ranger station when Jake became sheriff—but it's home base for our small team. Four deputies total, covering the town and surrounding mountains. Not enough if real trouble comes.

The main room is empty except for Lisa at dispatch, tapping away at her computer while simultaneously filing her nails into lethal points. She raises an eyebrow as I enter.

"You look like you ate something that disagreed with you," she says, not looking up from her nails. "Bad morning?"

"Weird morning," I correct her, hanging my jacket on the hook by the door. "Is Jake in?"

She jerks her chin toward the back office. "Coffee's fresh too. Might improve your mood."

I grunt my thanks and pour a cup of black coffee before heading to Jake's office. The door's open, but I knock anyway—old habits from when he was just my best friend's scary older brother, not my boss.

Jake looks up from a pile of paperwork, reading glasses perched on his nose. He might be sheriff now, but the alpha authority that radiates off him hasn't changed since he was twenty. It's why Sanctuary works—why omegas feel safe here. Jake doesn't let shit slide.

"Got your message," he says, gesturing for me to close the door. "What's up at the school?"

I set my coffee down and lower myself into the chair across from his desk. "Someone's been scoping it out. Found tracks along the fence line, like they were testing for weak spots."

Jake's expression darkens. "Any evidence it's connected to the reports from Mrs. Atkins?"

"Can't confirm, but timing fits." I rub the back of my neck, trying to organize my thoughts. "Found a kid's mitten there too. Probably nothing, but the scent on it was... off. Unfamiliar."

"Off how?"

"Not local. Not like any of the packs I know around here." I hesitate. "Sharp. Aggressive. The kind that makes your hackles rise."

Jake removes his glasses, pinching the bridge of his nose. "Shit. Last thing we need is territory trouble this close to winter."

"I've arranged extra patrols. Collins and Martinez will swing by during drop–off and pickup times." I take a sip of coffee, grimacing at the bitterness. "The school's going to be a problem if this prowler shows up again."

"You think they're targeting the school specifically?"

I consider this, remembering the deliberate nature of those tracks, how they followed the fence line exactly where the playground sits. "Yeah. I do. Question is why? Most of the kids are from established families. Local pack kids or human. Few omegas that young."

"Any new enrollments recently?" Jake asks.

"Don't know. But there's a new staff member. Woman. Didn't get her name." I try to keep my voice neutral, but something in Jake's expression tells me I've failed.

"You catch her scent?" he asks, too casually.

I scowl. "Not relevant."

"Funny, I didn't ask if it was relevant." His mouth quirks up at the corner. "I asked if you caught it."

"Yeah." My voice comes out rougher than intended. "Omega. Strong."

Jake leans back in his chair, the wood creaking under his weight. The knowing look on his face makes me want to bare my teeth.

"Don't," I warn.

"Didn't say anything." He holds up his hands in mock surrender. "Though it's interesting that you immediately got defensive."

"I'm not—" I cut myself off, jaw clenching. "Look, the point is, something's not right. Someone's circling that school, and my instincts say it's not for a parent-teacher conference."

Jake nods, mercifully dropping the subject of the omega teacher. "I'll call Principal Wilson, see what he knows about new students or staff. You follow up on the scent trail. If it doesn't match any locals, we need to figure out who's new in town."

"Already on it." I stand, draining the last of my coffee. "I've got the mitten in an evidence bag in my car."

"Good work." Jake picks up his phone, effectively dismissing me. "Oh, and Finn?"

I pause at the door, looking back.

"Maybe introduce yourself to the new teacher. Professionally. If there's potential trouble brewing, all staff should be on alert."

I grunt noncommittally and step out, closing the door a bit harder than necessary. The thought of seeing that teacher again—of getting closer to that scent—sends a ripple of something dangerous down my spine. For her sake, it's better if I keep my distance.

But as I head back to my desk to file the report, my mind keeps circling back to her—the way she hummed to herself in the cold, the brief flash of her eyes meeting mine, the scent that somehow cut through pine and winter and wrapped around something deep inside me.

Something's coming—I can feel it. And for reasons I refuse to examine, the thought of that humming-soft teacher being caught in the middle sets my teeth on edge.

Learn more about Finn and Jenny's story in The Alpha Deputy!

ALSO BY ASH JADE

Read more from Ash Jade
Short, binge-worthy omegaverse romances where instinct burns hot and love always wins.

Lost Ridge Riders Universe

Welcome to Lost Ridge.
Where the roads are long, the walls are guarded,
and no omega is ever owned—only chosen.

Salt and Timber Coast Universe

Welcome to the Salt & Timber Coast.
*A rain-bound peninsula where protection is
steady, bonds are chosen, and love means staying.*

Blackwater Bears

*A quiet inland pack where bear shifters offer
shelter, endurance, and a home that holds.*

The Starfall Ridge Quick Reads Series

Welcome to Starfall Ridge.
*Where the crater sparks scents, fate strikes fast,
and no one escapes the pull of a mate.*

The Yule Curse Series

*Four fated nights. Four cursed alphas. One winter
where heat burns brighter than fire.*

The Touch Her and Die Series

*In a world ruled by dominance, instinct, and the
pull of fate, every story begins with danger—and
ends with devotion.*

<u>The Sanctuary Pack Series</u>

Welcome to Sanctuary.
A hidden mountain town where omegas come to heal—and alphas learn what it means to protect.

ABOUT ASH JADE

Ash Jade writes trope-packed omegaverse romances full of heat, ruts, and fated mates — but always with heart. Her stories are fast, messy, and addictive, blending primal passion with emotional cores that make the bonds hit even harder. If you love bingeable romances where instinct tangles with feelings (and always ends in happily-ever-after), you've found your pack.

ashjadeauthor.com

www.ingramcontent.com/pod-product-compliance
Lightning Source LLC
Chambersburg PA
CBHW021129070726
47591CB00014B/1944